LAIR RISING

LAIR
2

D.V. SULLIVAN

TP

TRANSMARINIA PRESS

ISBN for ebook: 979-8-9866781-2-2
ISBN for paperback: 979-8-9866781-4-6
First Published February 2024, 2nd Edition August 2024

For readers 18+. Contains brief descriptions of domestic violence.

Cover design by Trif Book Design.

Transmarinia Press
2709 N Hayden Island Dr
STE 330550
Portland, OR 97217

*To the person in you
who decided
to rise up*

ONE

I prop myself up on the sunbed and fling my head back, drinking in the warmth of Southern France.

Fuck me, life is good.

It seems only yesterday that I was back in rainy Oregon, splitting my days between wrestling yearlings on the farm and pouring shots at the local bar. That couldn't be more removed from this glamorous lifestyle of cruising sun-kissed seas and lazing on far-flung beaches. A dizzying gratitude brims up in me, and I lift the coconut shell out of the baking sand by my side and take a sip of my piña colada. Who says dreams never come true?

Every dream has its price, though.

I finger my cocktail straw and look about. The crowds have changed only marginally, if at all. I'd never before heard of Club 55, but apparently you have to book months in advance, if you can even afford it in the first place. It's cute, with its quaint white chairs and blue table linens fluttering under the palm trees.

It also happens to be a favorite hotspot for the world's rich and famous.

They cover Pampelonne Beach in an oily glistening of skin. Over here sculpted movie stars canoodling with pop singers. Over there hairy-shouldered business magnates turned crimson with sunburn, their physical decline not stopping impossibly beautiful, leggy girls from draping themselves over them. My insides constrict in disgust. How artificial can you get?

I don't let this spoil my mood, though. It's hard not to soak in all this perfect summer glitz and glamour. The water sparkles, young flesh gleams, guests are ferried to and fro from the restaurant's private jetty to the fleet of megayachts waiting offshore.

In fact, one arrives as I watch.

I pull my sunglasses down my nose and squint. A distinguished man in his fifties, in a billowy cream shirt and close-cropped silver hair, departing from a yacht with *Wet Dream* emblazoned on its transom. I compare him to the photo on my phone, and it's an exact match.

Bingo.

My hands are shaking as I gather my hair up in a ponytail and tug at the strings of my bikini top, making sure my breasts are front-and-center attention grabbers. Will it be enough? As I strut across the coal-hot sands, I pass a pair of supermodels in colorful wraps prowling for their millionaires and they give me a cold once-over, lips pursed in jealousy and scorn.

That would be a yes, then. They know competition when they see it, after all.

May the best bitch win.

I never let the new arrival stray from my sight, and so I find him before any of the other girls have time to descend upon him. He's staked out a sunbed beneath a striped parasol, and already a waiter has scurried out from the restaurant with a kitschy umbrella cocktail; he's a regular. Also, alone. Perhaps he left the wife behind for this little trip.

He takes his cocktail, sips it, and tosses it into the sand, his imprecations sending the waiter scurrying back for a replacement.

Ah, yes. Remember what else you were told about him?

(History of violence: assault and battery. Be careful.)

All right, Aurora. Showtime.

As I approach, he lifts his shirt over his head in preparation for a swim. He has a tight swell of belly, the body of a man who was once muscular but whose ambitions have usurped all other interests in life. A hard mouth that speaks to harder appetites.

It's even easier than I thought it would be. When I saunter by him with hips swaying, I make sure to stumble and let him catch me, letting out a mortified little gasp. "Oh my God," I gush. "I'm *so* sorry."

We both snort a sociable, declarative and slightly apologetic laugh, the kind that communicates a great many things.

From there, the conversation leads itself.

"You all right?"

"Yeah. Wow, I'm not usually this awkward . . ."

"That's all right. Usually women lose their balance *after* I smile at them."

And he is smiling, waiting for my surprised and delighted laugh. His cool, appraising look— somehow more considerate and intimate than any that might pass between a married couple— gives me a chill.

And then the inevitable question: "Are you alone?"

Night has fallen by the time we stagger through ochre-colored streets to the port of St. Tropez.

Ahead, the sleek silhouettes of yachts loom tall. Ahead, dark and waiting, the *Lair*.

I've learned a great deal about my companion by now. He's in the arms business, and he likes to own things. His name (which he never tells me) is listed on the registers for some of the most expensive possessions in the world, and so I've taken to calling him Grubby Hands in my head.

He is that, too. He's frat boy drunk (I am tipsy but feigning drunkenness), and he won't stop grabbing at my ass as we lurch up the passerelle. I suppress a shiver of revulsion and swat his hand away, jaw hanging in girlish shock. *"Bad boy!"*

He leers. "Isn't that how you like 'em?"

God, this whole performance of mine is abhorrent. I detest it.

But I'm almost there.

I snicker and screw a finger through the air at him. "You're a little spoiled, aren't you?"

"Who doesn't like being spoiled?" he smirks and effects a sloppy salute for the silver-haired man waiting on the aft main deck. The man is tall, broad-shouldered for his age, in a white polo with the anchor and four gold stripe epaulettes of a captain. Arnold Redfearn and I lock eyes, and he scans the empty waterfront before pressing a button. There's a whir and the passerelle lifts, begins to sheathe into itself and retract away from the dock. Grubby Hands looks back at this, frowning with great concentration . . . and sniggers like a schoolboy. "You don't want me leaving, do you?"

"That's right," I say, and tug him by his shirt inside the *Lair*.

He keeps bumping into the walls as we tiptoe through the dark yacht, and I shush him. We've taken to giggling like teenagers sneaking into a parents' house. He lifts his brows when we pass through red-stained double doors into the master suite, taking in the soaring walls with their crimson canvases and light-absorbing panels. "Your boyfriend has quite the boat . . ."

"Yes. He does."

"And you're sure he won't be back tonight?"

I cock my head and narrow my eyes, giving him a slow, sexy smile as I pull him toward the enormous bed. "Don't tell me you haven't broken any rules before . . ."

He grins as I push him down. "Maybe."

"Maybe," I repeat, and cock a hip. "Uh-huh."

He shrugs. "If you're rich, you can get away with anything."

I arch a brow and touch a corner of my mouth with my tongue. "Like?"

He laces his hands behind his head and blinks up at me as if from a great distance. "You're a dark one, aren't you?"

I crawl onto the bed and over him, offering him a front-row view of my assets, and say the word as if tasting a strawberry: "Yes."

His teeth show in a vicious grin, excitement glowing like a fever in his eyes. He lunges up to kiss me, but I stop him with the tips of two fingers over his mouth. "Talk first. It turns me on to hear all the horrible things you bad boys do.

He lofts a brow. "You *are* a dark one."

"*Talk*," I command, and push him down.

He chuckles from behind clenched teeth and fists his hands into the sheets as he stares up at the ceiling, writhing, khaki shorts straining over his arousal. I obediently pluck at his belt buckle.

"Well," he explains when he's regained some measure of control. "If you're a yacht owner, responsibility is optional. The rules don't apply to you. So if my crew pisses me off I can just confiscate their passports and withhold their wages."

My hands pause at his belt. "That's it?" I scoff. "I thought you'd be badder than that . . ."

His eyes narrow, anger mixing with a deep, dangerous lust at this challenge. "All right. Say you have a deckhand who's exhausted after working back-to-back shifts. He's cleaning the yacht at night, and the dumb shit falls and cracks his head, drowns in the harbor?" He shrugs. "You can just lift anchor and leave, pay to have some other boat hire divers to search for the kid's body and deal with the police. We had to go pick up a porn star that day anyway."

My hands are trembling as I snick out his belt. "Must be a thrill to know the authorities can't touch you."

He nods, counting the freckles in my cleavage. "But I can touch anyone I want. So if I like the look of a stewardess, well . . ." And his tongue runs along the tops of his teeth as he looks in my eyes.

There's a plummeting in my gut, an immense settling.

I suck in a shivery breath. "So," I say, hovering over him, letting my parted lips graze close, and begin to cuff his wrists over his head with the belt. "You like hurting women, do you?"

He nods, delirious, eyes glazed with desire. "Yes."

"Good," I whisper, knotting the belt tail tight around a bedpost, and smile a dazzling smile. "Because I like hurting men who hurt women." His face, for the first time, tightens in confusion. "What?"

A tension gathers in the air. I'm off the bed now, backing away. My heart is hammering, my nerves buzzing in my skin, but I can set this aside—because the decision has been made. Gradually, I begin to feel more at peace with what's about to happen.

I place my hands on my hips and eye him askance. "You didn't really think there was no one like me out there, did you? If you're going to abuse that many women, the least you can do is have the courtesy to assume that, one day, one of them was going to abuse you right back."

He colors, almost too astounded to be offended. "*What* did you say?"

"Oh, and I *may* have told you a teensy little lie or two," I say, lifting a finger. "You see, he's here, actually. On the boat." The corners of my mouth widen: *eek*. "Sorry."

The man is yanking on the belt when he hears this. He stills. "Who's here?" Then his head jerks as he senses something in the gloom. The pitch of his voice rises. "W-who's there?"

"He's not very good at being patient," I confess and cock my head, studying the man as if he were an insect pinned wriggling to a wall. "Especially when he's hungry."

It's in this moment that Adrian Voper appears at my side, gliding out of the shadows along the walls.

The man tied to the bed goes rigid, the breath panting in and out of him, too stricken to move. "What the—what is—" He swallows, blinking through a thick haze of alcohol, and spreads the fingers of his bound hands. "Look, man, I didn't know she was your—"

"Yes, you did," I say.

"Okay, whatever. I can give you—I have so much money—"

"We don't want your money," I say, and look over at Adrian as he flows closer. "Money isn't red . . ."

That's when Grubby Hands takes in the corpse-white pallor of Adrian's skin, and his teeth, and the cold hunger in his eyes, and an ancient fear brushes against his heart. "Please," he whispers, throat bobbing. "Please don't . . ."

I turn away as the screaming begins.

Later, as I face the wall trembling and arms crossed, we talk. Adrian is splashed red, shoulders hunched in shame and contrition.

"You okay?" he ventures.

I clear my throat. "Yeah. It's just . . . getting harder."

He sighs. "Babe, you don't have to do this. We can find another way—"

"Can we?" I shake my head. "I don't want you hunting women anymore, and right now you're too weak to go after men on your own. So whether we like it or not, this is our only option."

"You seducing criminals?" he growls. "Yeah, can't say I'm a big fan of that part, either."

I rub my forehead. "Don't worry about it. I'm fine.

I can feel his eyes on me, sensing I need reassurance. "He *was* a criminal, Aurora," he reminds me. "A *rapist*. The courts couldn't touch him. You did the world a service." His voice is low, soothing, tinged with fear. "I'll have my strength back after this, and I'll be able to hunt on my own again." He sits back against the bed and places his elbows on his knees, swipes a wet trickle from the corner of his mouth and looks at the blood dripping from his long, tapered hands. His feeding over the past couple of weeks has begun to fill him out, upgraded him from the emaciated corpse look he's been rocking since he tried starving himself for me, but he is still jarringly thin compared to the old Adrian.

What he says next, I know, is as much for himself as it is for me. "We just need to do this for a little longer. After Volok is gone, we'll be free of this. Forever."

I turn to look at him then, the disgust on his face, and something in me crumples. I kneel beside him and hug him hard about the neck as he sits there, eyes shut.

"We'll get through this. We will. I promise."

He nods, jaw muscles dancing. Nods again.

"I'll never leave your side, do you understand?" I whisper it fiercely, a brutal promise. "I love you, Adrian."

I sense his body relax against mine. "I love you, too." Then, his voice hoarse, "I can't say how grateful I am that you're doing this for me."

Emotion swells my throat shut. I pull back, dashing a wrist over my eyes, and stare at the bloodless corpse on the bed. I blurt it out before I'm even aware of what I'm saying. "We need to change the crew."

He turns to me. "What?"

"Strip the *Lair* down to a skeleton crew. This is no longer a pleasure boat, is it?"

Adrian swallows. "No."

"We can't be like them." I gesture at the bed. "We can't treat our crew like they treat theirs. And if it ever gets dangerous, going after Volok, they need to be kept out of it. Agreed?"

He looks at me, a wisp of an admiring smile about his lips. "Agreed."

"Good." I stand and offer a hand. After a moment, he places his sticky one in mine, and allows me to pull him to his feet. "So," I say when he's wavering before me, and shake my hair out of my face. "Who's going to tell Mrs. Colding?"

TWO

Mrs. Colding clasps her hands before her and peers out the sloping windows of the wheelhouse with narrowed eyes.

Captain Redfearn, arms crossed over his epauletted polo, leans against the glowing nav consoles and eyes the chief stewardess with the respectful air of a man who knows not to poke a bear. Beside me, Adrian watches her. I watch her. All around us, the Mediterranean night presses close in blocks of darkness, as if it too were waiting on her words.

When they come they are as dry as toast. "So you're going to hunt down and destroy your maker, who also happens to be the head of your coven and the most powerful vampire in the world."

Adrian nods. "Yes."

"So you can turn back into a human."

"Yes."

"Even if it takes picking off a swath of undead to do it." Adrian gulps. "Yes."

And Mrs. Colding takes us in, the faintest trace of a smile twitching her mouth. "Well, it's about bloody time."

Adrian deflates in relief, shaking his head. I find I'm grinning ear to ear.

"Before we go any further," Mrs. Colding cautions, drawing herself up, "we need to be clear with each other. This'll be no walk in the park. We will be hunting down creatures that have crawled out of legend. Even if we see it through, we will be different people afterward. So I want to hear it from all of you. After this there's no turning back."

"Of course," Adrian agrees.

"I think you know where I stand," I say.

"Captain?" Mrs. Colding turns to Redfearn.

The grizzled skipper shrugs his broad shoulders. "Sure beats retirement."

The four of us stand there, grinning like idiots.

"So," I say at last, rubbing my hands together. "Where do we start?"

All heads turn to Adrian, who slowly smiles. "By having an old friend over for a chat."

It's sunrise as I watch the *Vespertine*'s limo tender glide toward the *Lair*.

The stern has been opened to flood the beach club into a marina, and I wait at its edge as the tender approaches, the sun a shimmering disc of golden fire behind it. I can't see the tender's passenger yet; it has a sleek coach roof hiding whoever's within from the beating sun. But I know what awaits me. I had a whole sleepless night to think about it.

I scan my surroundings. We're anchored off Cap Ferrat with its opulent villas set back amongst the umbrella pines along the shoreline, and so when I take in a deep breath to settle my nerves, I scent salt and pine on the air, and something else—the barest, most understated of perfumes, evocative and sophisticated.

Mrs. Colding is standing beside me.

She's as impeccable as ever. Her dark hair is pulled tightly back into a bun, her elegant black skirt and white button-down as crisp as ice. Her expression on her ageless Chinese features is the usual: the self-satisfied smirk of a queen in her kingdom, as if she had the balls of every person in the room held hostage in her purse. Lady balls included.

I squeeze my thighs together.

"I knew you'd be trouble," she murmurs. "But this . . ." Her mouth seams in a closed-lipped smile.

My stomach does a little flip. "I was nervous to tell you."

"Oh?"

I edge a look at Adrian brooding nearby with hands in pockets, hard blue eyes fixed on the approaching tender boat. He's changed into a suit, which he only wears now during times of business with his kind, to keep up appearances. Another thing he let go of for me. "You've known him for so long, I didn't know if—"

But she dismisses this. "Nonsense. You've proven you know what's best for him."

My chest swells with an unexpected thrill of validation. "Thank you."

The chief stewardess purses her lips. "And you've thought this through? The possibilities? There's a very real chance this will not go your way. Adrian could die trying to pull this off. Or you could die and he'd switch to feeding on brunettes until the end of time . . ."

I snort, twisting an end of my dark hair. "I know. But I don't think I could stay with him otherwise." My voice lowers. "And I couldn't bear to not be with him."

Mrs. Colding nods, taking this in. "All right, then." And as the tender boat glides like a shark into the shaded safety of the marina lapping inside the *Lair*, she clasps her hands before her. "Just be careful. We're in dangerous waters here."

Yes. Yes, indeed.

When I look up Adrian is standing beside me, pale face serious. "Ready?"

As I ever will be.

And then deckhands are tossing mooring lines through the air, and a figure in a close-fitting suit emerges from the enclosed cabin of the tender boat. Tall, lean, possessed of haughty grace, long pale hands adjusting cuff links. The hands spread, and Anatoly Anatolovich smiles a sharp and satirical and chillingly cunning smile. "My old friend," he calls out. "What was so pressing that we had to meet in this horrid daytime hour?"

THREE

Anatoly doesn't let up on his complaints of the sun, wincing as if at a migraine, and so Adrian leads us toward the VIP guest suites. Of course, we had expected this.

Mrs. Colding remains behind in the beach club. When I look back at her, she is watching us go with her body rigidly composed, mouth clamped tight. She nods at me. *Good luck.*

Adrian opens the door to the first guest suite and gestures inside. He had it prepared especially for our use, ordering the few portholes to be battened down with storm covers, casting the clean, modern space with its glossy wood panels into a cool and inviting dimness. Anatoly sighs in relief, gliding through the gloom to sink onto a sofa upholstered in flesh-toned kidskin. "This is better," he says, pinching the bridge of his nose.

Adrian and I stand close for a moment, hands brushing against each other as if for encouragement.

We seat ourselves carefully on the other end of the sweeping sofa, and I arrange the skirt of my light summer dress, bare legs crossed. When Anatoly boldly appraises me, as if for the first time taking in my purpose and sexuality, I feel my neck and face grow hot, slightly perspiring.

"My, my," he muses aloud. "She's still here."

I meet his gaze, tightening my jaw so my teeth won't chatter. An awful dryness has sealed my throat. "She is."

Beyond this, I think. *I should be beyond this. Look how far I've come.*

You don't scare me.

Oh, but he does. He certainly does.

Anatoly's eyes crinkle. "And here I was, thinking I scared you off the first time we met."

I lift my chin and force my voice steady as I grit it out. "I think you'll find it takes more than you to scare me off."

His lips crimp in amusement before he turns to Adrian. "I can see why you haven't . . . *enjoyed* her yet." That word in his mouth is not soft, as most people think it to be, but cruel and tearing. "You do plan to, don't you?"

Adrian's hands clench into fists on his thighs. "No."

"Ah," Anatoly intones, a whole world expressed in that exhalation. "I see." His eyes return to me, marveling. "She is impressive, I grant you. But still. A pet, Voper. A pet. Should I be concerned?"

The sweat is pearling on my upper lip now. A deep flush attacks my face, giving me away.

But Adrian beside me says nothing.

The anger comes off him in waves, ice cold and controlled—for the moment. I slip my hand into one of the fists on his thighs, and he grips it tight.

Anatoly's teeth, long and yellow as a lemon peel, glint in a smile. "You always were different, Voper. I've always liked that about you." He crosses one leg over the other and leans back, eyes glittering. "So. Why am I here?"

Adrian gives me a sidelong look before saying it. "I'd like to speak with the Commodore." The name buzzes in the air, lifting one of Anatoly's brows. "Oh?" But he does not look up, brushing casually at a pant leg. "Why is that?"

"It's been . . . some time. Since I've showed my fealty."

Anatoly nods at this. "Indeed it has. You have not let the Commodore feed on you in . . . five years? More? If you were not the *Commodore's* pet, that sort of defiance would not go unpunished. But he has a soft spot for you, as we all know."

I glance at Adrian. Fealty? These nightfolk feeding on each other? A whole world. A whole, unsettling world I am still not privy to. *We'll be speaking about this later, Adrian.*

Anatoly lifts his eyes. "Why the change of heart, Voper?"

The pause is the briefest of moments, but it is enough. Lines appear in Anatoly's forehead. His voice deepens in wonder and admiration. "You want to kill him, don't you? You're in love with this plaything, and you . . ." The bark of laughter comes now, he cannot hold it back. He holds a fist to his mouth, looks at Adrian and laughs again, holds up a hand. "Sorry, I am sorry. But my dear Voper, whatever are you doing?"

Adrian's voice is hard as bedrock. "You cannot tell me you're happy being this way."

"Actually . . ."

"We're murderers, Anatoly."

Anatoly lifts a clarifying finger. "All the super-rich are murderers, Voper—opportunists sucking others dry. We're simply more literal about it." He leans forward, the corners of his mouth dimpling. "Voper, Voper, Voper. What did you let this mortal do to you?"

Adrian's jaw muscles flex. "I've never wanted to be this way." His hand is crushing mine now. "Aurora merely gave me the courage to see the way out."

Pride floods through me—but Anatoly does not share my sentiment.

"The way out," he says, as if examining the words, and shakes his head. He stands, pacing in the shadows of the suite, and runs a hand through his slicked-back hair. "You do remember what you're up against, yes?" To me he smirks, "Did he tell you?"

A coldness seeps into my bones.

"Volok . . . he is the devil, my dear. The Beast of Rusland, they called him in the old days. He is smoke, vapor. You will never find him. And even if you did . . ." My arms break out in gooseflesh as Anatoly laughs—insane, delighted laughter—and I turn to see Adrian's face slacken in doubt.

No.

Anatoly is reveling in his glee. "No. He will always outwit you. You will never find him, even if you—" And he chokes on the words, face mottling. Adrian's head jerks up.

"What?" I say, heart thudding. "What is it?"

Adrian's voice is hollow with revelation. "The Shipwright. Of course!" He stands, slow with thought, the beginnings of a restlessness overtaking him. "The builder of all the boats for our kind. The Shipwright knows every vessel, every owner. If there's one person who would know Volok's boat and his cruising grounds . . ." He turns to Anatoly.

The Easterner's sleek face has contorted into a snarl of rage.

The two vampires stand there, facing each other. The mood in the room has changed, grown charged. I feel as if a match were struck, the air would catch fire.

Adrian takes a breath. "You could help us, Anatoly. He turned you too, didn't he? We could both leave this behind."

But Anatoly straightens as if someone has made an unsavory pass at him, long nose constricting, nostrils flared. "I think we both know that won't happen."

"Yes," says Adrian in a flat voice. And then, "So what happens now?"

The room hums.

At last Anatoly settles his shoulders, jaw working. "Well," he remarks carefully, his tone blurred between spite and a sort of disgusted relinquishment. "I suppose you can't trust me to keep quiet, can you?"

No. No, we couldn't, Anatoly Anatolovich.

For we had thought this through the night before. Even if he didn't run off to inform Volok— out of fear of reprisal or rousing Volok's wrath—there was the possibility he would merely return to take care of the situation himself, perhaps with the help of a friend. *(I know where his boat is anchored. He'll never expect it.)* If not tomorrow night, then the next, or the next after that, they would rise dripping out of the sea and climb aboard the *Lair*, long pale shadows gliding into the master suite and over our bed . . .

Can't have that.

"No. We can't," I say, rising, and Anatoly's eyes flick to me. "That's why we planned for it." And lifting the iPad in my hand, I tap a button.

Anatoly sneers as if I'm trying out a trick that won't work. But then he hears the *clunk* behind him, a hydraulic whir, and he snaps around to look.

An outline of golden light is appearing in the guest suite's outboard wall. For the wall has begun to *move*, folding out from the *Lair* into a private outdoor balcony, and sunshine blazes inside with annihilating force.

When Anatoly whirls back he is seething with betrayal, canines lengthened like a cornered animal's. His eyes dart to Adrian, who is now standing in the dark passageway outside the door to the suite, and I hold up the iPad and wave. "Enjoy the view, Anatolovich." I smile. "It's killer."

And I dash for the door.

There's a wild moment of panic as I hear him snarl after me, and a matter-of-fact voice inside me says, *He can't catch you. You have too much of a head start.* And still—his fiendish white face is right there when I turn and help Adrian slam the door shut. Something crashes into it on the other side and it jumps in its frame, but holds. I suck in air, not having taken a real breath in a long time, and turn to Adrian. "Jesus," I whisper, and shriek as Anatoly's clawed hand punches through the door.

I fall and scramble back on all fours, chest heaving and one dress strap slipping off my shoulder as I gape at the hand straining at the air. The skin on it is a shiny black, pulled tight over the bone as from a nasty burn, and within seconds it's crisping and fuming up smoke. There's a shout from within the room, a hair-raising scream, and a waft of fire blazes along the coat sleeve, licking through the door and bringing the stench of burnt flesh to my nostrils.

That's when the howling begins.

I clap my hands over my ears and turn away, eyes welling, and they are still there by the time the howls stop and the charred claw has crumbled to a heap of ash on the carpet.

FOUR

The coverup is clean and efficient. It's regretfully expressed to the *Vespertine*'s captain that there's been an accident. A fall overboard, alcohol involved. Of course, divers will be hired to search for the body. But it would be appreciated if the *Lair* and Adrian's name were kept out of the news. (Bad business, a blot on the boat's reputation, et cetera.) An envelope thick with euros is exchanged to help with the decision.

The *Vespertine*'s captain, pale and trembling and looking as if he's been released from some waking nightmare, makes no objections.

At least, this is what Adrian and I are told later that evening as we recline on sun loungers on the top deck as the Jacuzzi fills, Captain Redfearn and Mrs. Colding updating us as if they were officers in a general's tent. Adrian nods in satisfaction when they've finished, and Captain Redfearn adds in summation, "It could have gone worse, all things considered."

"And it almost did," Mrs. Colding snips. "Our luck won't hold out if we keep this up." Captain Redfearn surveys the tops of his deck shoes, his thick arms crossed. "Maybe." Then, "Are we really going to the Shipwright?"

Adrian stares out at the darkly glittering sea as he says it. "Thinking it's a bad idea, Arnold?" The captain exchanges an *Are you kidding me?* look with Mrs. Colding, and he's opened his mouth in argument when a deckhand pops up to switch off the Jacuzzi pump. The captain pokes the inside of his cheek with his tongue, hands on hips, and looks off. But when the deckhand mutters a meek "Excuse me" and dips away, the captain only bows his silver head and growls, "I'll chart a course north." And with that he slips past.

Mrs. Colding, however, lingers to look me up and down, clearly having noted my lack of participation in all this. "You all right?"

I wince a smile. "Just tired, thanks."

She lingers a moment longer, eyeing me. Then inclines her head and is gone, a slender shadow disappearing into the darkness beyond the nimbus of light wavering out of the Jacuzzi. When her footsteps have faded, I notice Adrian studying me with his vivid blue eyes. "*Are* you all right?"

I draw in a long, shivery breath, thinking of Anatoly's shrieks as his body became an inferno, and let it out. "I'm not sure."

Adrian reaches out to touch my arm. "We can stop here. This doesn't have to go any further."

"I know." I can tell he's not satisfied with this, and to head off any further probing I say, "You didn't tell me that Volok was . . . is he really that bad?"

Adrian frowns, but indulges me. "He's the oldest of us, and the first to take to the sea. He has had many names, taken many forms. He's so ancient he no longer looks like a man. He has become something . . . *other*."

The backs of my arms prickle with a chill.

"He created our way of life," Adrian goes on. "Our kind, we are a proud bunch—we do not like change. Why leave what we had known for centuries? But we saw the wisdom in Volok's plan. Our world was shrinking, growing smaller. It was time to adapt. And so we did. Volok was the one who founded Lair Yachting Incorporated, the yacht club—"

I stare. "A *yacht club?* They have a fucking—" I shut my eyes, fingertips to temples. "Of course they do. Of *course* they do."

Adrian, greatly entertained, bites back a smile. "That's why Volok is called the Commodore—it's what yacht clubs call their chairman. It amuses him to indulge these little traditions. You may have seen our flag." He points a finger skyward, and I crane my head up at the *Lair*'s radar arch with its blinking lights and puffy white radomes. Something snaps in the wind from a starboard antenna—something I've seen before. It's the triangular pennant I watched Jason, the former first mate, hoist when Anatoly first visited the *Lair*. All-black save for a pair of inverted white triangles, looking almost like an abstract, geometric representation of . . .

Oh. Right.

"A burgee," Adrian explains. "A yacht club's unique flag. It's how we recognize one another."

"And this fealty?"

Adrian's lips thin. "It's what Volok demands of the coven, to show his mastery over us."

"He *feeds* on you."

A nod.

I think of many suited men standing in a line, each waiting their turn to kneel before a sharp-toothed shadow on a throne, and shiver. "So why does he let you get away with defying him?"

Adrian drops his gaze, shrugs. "As strong as his obsession for obedience is . . . there are things that even he fears."

I don't know what to make of that. What is he hinting at?

Whatever. Glampires and their empires.

I jump up. "I don't know about you, but I'm ready for a dip."

A faint scowl appears around Adrian's mouth—he knows I'm still avoiding him. So I untie the knot of my shirt with sharp, coquettish movements, eyes locked on him, and when I lift it over my head I fling it at him in my best imitation of a cowgirl. It hits his face and tumbles off him, and he snorts, rises to join me.

That's right.

Grinning, I unzip my tiny cut-off jean shorts, shimmy them down my hips, and stepping out of them in nothing but my bikini I tiptoe, giggling and shrieking, into the Jacuzzi. It's gloriously hot. "Oh my *God*," I groan, hugging myself and shivering at that familiar pins and needles sensation. "*This* is what I needed!"

But Adrian, standing in his swimming trunks at the rim, has his shirt unbuttoned but still on. I tilt my head, smiling. "It's *okaaay*," I tease. "I still love you with your nosferatu bod."

He smirks again and looks down. Jesus, he'd somehow be even more handsome if he was alive to blush.

Then he shrugs his shirt off.

"Oh," I find myself saying, feeling my jaw hang in what can only be described as a gape. That last infusion of blood must have done the trick, for he no longer looks shrink-wrapped, gaunt with unnatural malnourishment. On the contrary, he looks bigger than he ever has, muscles puffed up and healthy, his chest broader than a pick-up truck. Even his inner forearms pop with those little muscly veins that bodybuilders have. In short, his body is *smoking*.

"Something wrong?" he says with curved lips as he descends into the Jacuzzi.

I shake my head. "Nope. Definitely not."

He has a full-on smirk now as he looms over me. "Have I made a full recovery, then?"

I gulp, nodding. "This doctor certainly thinks so."

He arches a brow. "Your official diagnosis?"

I lay a hand on the hard square of one pec, feeling the power thrumming beneath it, and breathe, "Hubba hubba."

He's still smiling when he kisses me.

His lips are firm, and smooth, and cool, and it's only now that I appreciate how much I've missed them. We haven't been intimate in a while, not since that first time outside the *Lair*'s master suite. What with everything that's happened—the guilty, confusing roil of emotions, his starvation and weakness, our hunting—there's simply been no room for it. But the tension has been building again, along with my curiosity. And now . . .

I pull away, and we lock eyes for a moment before I put my hands against the exciting solidity of his abs and push him down. His perfect brow furrows, and then I'm rising up over him, slinky and seductive, water channeling down my body as I straddle him in one smooth movement. His blue-black eyes go wide with surprise. When I arch my back to settle more fully onto him, gyrating ever so slightly in his lap, I'm rewarded with the feel of him against me. He's as hard as a rock.

"Oh," he breathes. It comes out choked and husky. "I see."

I run a hand through my wet mane of hair, dragging it out of the way, and dip my head to kiss him. It's a declaration. An order. *I need this*, my lips tell him. *I've been craving it. And I want to know. I want to know if it will be as amazing as the first time.*

Apparently, this message gets through loud and clear. His hands, which had come to a surprised rest on my hips, grip into flesh. He groans into my mouth, and when I begin to grind against him, rising slowly up and down against the long length of him inside his swimming trunks, he looks down at our hips with lips parted, a dazed expression on his face. "Fuck."

I'm trembling all over now. A desperate, blinding need has taken possession of me. I reach behind me to undo the strings of my bikini top, and when it slides off my breasts my nipples are already perked and waiting. He dutifully sucks on one—hungrily, ravenously—and I hold his head there, gasping, a heavy ache between my legs now.

Yeah. *Fuck* is right.

I grip the scruff of his hair and pull his head back to kiss him full on the mouth. Hard. He grips my ass, guiding my grinding hips, and a low, angry noise escapes me.

This is what I've wanted. This is what we've needed.

This is how you feel alive.

The world lurches, and Adrian rises with my legs wrapped around him and whirls me about, water thrashing and slopping onto the deck. I'm suddenly slammed against a slick, angular surface and my elbows are propped on the rim of the Jacuzzi, breasts thrust out and heaving. In one single, brutal movement Adrian rips away my bikini bottom in a tearing of fabric and I gasp, feeling a fluttery tingling between my legs and a breathless squeezing of my heart. God, I'm ready for him.

I'm on fire for it, writhing for it, arching my hips, my stomach tight and aching. *Please, please,* I think. *I'll do anything for you, be anything for you. Just please don't make me wait any longer* . . . And I bite my lip and look sultrily up at him, legs spread in invitation as he looms over me, all glistening muscle and sharp-cheeked, sharp-mouthed face lit from below like some horror icon out of an old movie . . .

Oh.

And I feel it happen, slowly but surely. The familiar blurring, the sickening replacement. Not his face any longer. Not my lover's face at all.

It is Josh's face. My ex, Josh, looking down at me.

And with it, an unwelcome cascade of memory: Josh, sweaty and short of breath, cursing at me to shut up as he braces himself over me, teeth gritted as he yanks my legs wide . . .

No.

Hands reach out, long and pale and strong, to grip me by the hips and pull me close, and my stomach drops.

"Wait!"

Adrian freezes, that beautiful face of his drawn in confusion. "What is it?"

"I'm sorry," I say, shrinking away, one hand flying to my brow. "I'm sorry, I can't—" And then I'm wading to the other end of the bubbling pool, still throbbing—confoundingly—with desire, and turn away to hug my chest. I've broken out in goosebumps, trembling all over. My teeth are chattering. I'm so embarrassed I could just die.

"I guess I'm just not ready yet," is what I try to say, thinking I'm speaking normally. Then I become aware of my hitching, uncontrollable stuttering.

"I—I—I'm just—"

And he's there, lifting his arms in a comforting way, and before I know it they're about me, holding me, one hand rubbing my back. "It's all right," he soothes. "It's okay."

And it is, for a moment. It's hard not to be when I'm in his arms.

Then my stomach lurches.

"I'm sorry," I say again, grabbing a towel and wrapping it about me as I stumble out of the pool. I almost slip on the wet deck and he cringes, watching me. "I'm sorry, I have to go—"

"Aurora, please—"

But I'm gone. His agonized face floats away as I hurry down the stairs, nearly running now, as if I can somehow outrun the endless loop of Josh's voice in my head: *You belong to me. You'll always belong to me. You're* mine.

FIVE

The decks blur by in a streaking of mirrored glass and wood paneling. I'm padding through hallways toward the master suite, letting out little sniveling whimpers of anger and complaint. A stewardess watches me with round, alarmed eyes as I fling open one of the suite's red-stained doors. "Can I help you, miss—"

"NO!" I bellow and slam the door. She's still standing there with shoulders hunched up in petrified fright when I open it again. "A margarita, actually. And some chocolates." I pause. "Thank you." Then I slam the door again.

I can't block it out. Something has come loose, and my head is flooded with a swirl of memory, of what I thought I'd successfully buried and done away with: my life with Josh. The slights and breathlessly brusque dismissals, the injurious manipulations, the disgusted and theatrically reluctant recourses to violence. *(See what you've made me do? See?)*

It all flashes by like steeds on a runaway carousel, dizzying and terrifying. I have to put a stop to it, to put it all back where it was. I am pacing about and whimpering and hugging myself, wondering how.

The temptation to call my best friend Cailee is overwhelming. I grab my phone, my thumb hovering over her contact. But I can't. I can't drag her into this world. The last time I'd seen her, I'd made her promise to walk away from yachting—and the unnatural things she didn't know hid within it. But Cailee doesn't do not knowing. She's been calling and texting me constantly since *(You can't just disappear and expect me to not ask what's going on!)* and I've had to say this is something I just can't tell her. I know that if I open up now, it'd all just spill out, and she wouldn't be able to stay away. I'd only be endangering her. And I would never forgive myself for that.

I chuck my phone across the room.

I'm lying on the bed still in the towel when the door opens. I sniff back snot and sit up, wiping at my eyes. But it's not the stewardess. It's Mrs. Colding, standing in the doorway with a tray balanced on one hand and an understanding expression on her face. One exchanged look and I burst into tears.

"It's not *fair*," I whine, falling back and putting a pillow over my face. Mrs. Colding sets the tray on the nightstand and sits beside me. Before I know it, my head is in her lap. How has Mrs. Colding become my mom?

"What's not fair, dear?" she asks calmly.

I don't even hesitate. It all tumbles out. "I finally found someone I can—and every time we try to be intimate, I just see—"

"Your ex?"

"Yes," I sniff.

Mrs. Colding nods, thinking on that. She's smoothing my hair out over the bed with her hand, over and over, like a prayer. It's incredibly calming. "You're still in shock. And it's understandable that you'd draw that connection to other violent men. But Adrian is not your ex."

I nod, my cheek pressed into her skirt. "I know."

"He can't help his bloodlust."

I wipe at an eye. "But I don't know how long this will take to free him. And I can't just turn that part of me off until then."

The chief stewardess' voice is low and soothing. "You just need to give it time."

"I know, I just—I thought I'd be over this by now."

Mrs. Colding snorts above me. Not unkindly. It's more a grim acknowledgment of an infuriating fact in life.

"Trauma doesn't work that way, dear," she says at last, and the way she says it raises the goose bumps on my arms.

It's enough to goad me into one last confession.

"I'm afraid that a moment will come and I'll freeze," I whisper, so quiet there's no way anyone could hear me. "I'll freeze, like all the other times in my life, and I won't have what it takes to do what has to be done."

But Mrs. Colding hears. She looks down at me, seeking my eyes. "You had what it took today, didn't you?"

I screw up my nose, admitting it. "Yeah."

"Then you'll have it later when the time comes. Don't worry about that."

I sit up now to look into her eyes. I've never been this close to her. There's a stye at the corner of one eyelid, and I see that she uses something to darken her eyebrows. I don't know why—she's beautiful.

"You really think it's gonna be okay?" I whisper.

She smiles, the fine lines in her face spreading like a gentle cobweb, and tucks a lock of hair behind my ear. "As you two go on, and you see by his actions how different he is, it'll change. I promise."

"Okay." My voice is muted, pensive. I have a dim recognition of a change occurring, of crossing over into a new place with Mrs. Colding. Friendships between women had always been a mystery to me, how they come or how they last. But I suddenly realize this is one I desperately want to keep, and whose existence brings a blinding stab of gratitude to my eyes. Sometimes you just get lucky.

It takes me a moment to gather the courage to ask it—I have to blink back a sudden surge of tears. "When you said, you know, what you said about trauma . . . were you referring to what happened to Mr. Colding?"

A tightness enters her face, and her lips curve in a sad smile. "We'll talk about that sometime," she vows, patting my hand. "But not now." She passes me a shiny gift box of almond buttercrunch toffees and adds lightly, "I think you traumatized the new stewardess, though."

I hiccup a laugh. "Yeah." I pick out a chocolate and twirl it by its gold wrapper, turn and grip her hand. "Thank you, Mrs. Colding."

Those cobweb lines draw up. "Anytime, dear."

Later that night, Adrian slips quietly into bed. I can feel him watching me a moment before he turns over. My heart thumps in my chest. It's as if my body is filled with lead. But I break out of it. I roll up against his broad back and slip an arm around him, press my lips to the nape of his neck. As if that touch—long and trembling and tender—can inject hope into him. *Soon*, it says. *Soon.*

He takes in a big, shaky breath and lays his hand on top of mine, squeezes.

We fall asleep that way, with all available bare skin touching. My heart beating, red and strong, against the still and silent organ in his breast.

SIX

I wake to find he's gone, and startle upright.

But no, I tell myself. There's no reason to worry. It's been over a week now, cruising north, and I've only been dreaming of that night. Since then we've treated each other with the subdued respect of lovers reunited after a quarrel—pale and contrite, hushed with love, as if we had narrowly avoided some unspeakable disaster. So what has woken me now?

And then I hear the polite rap on the door. Mrs. Colding, standing in the dark hall bearing news. "We've arrived."

And we have. When I enter the wheelhouse, Adrian is there. He's in a sharp gray suit and stands with hands in pockets between a grim Mrs. Colding and Captain Redfearn at the helm. But they don't take notice of me. All their eyes are trained on what's looming out of wisps of early morning fog: an island. On it the spectral shapes of drably-colored cranes, slipways, dry docks, superyachts suspended in the enormous slings of hoisting cranes like godly infants in their swaddling. I don't know what to make of it. It's like a dream, this far-flung outpost clustered in the shadow of foreboding alps, like the kind of dread place that exists only at the edges of maps or in half-forgotten stories.

A shipyard.

"Where are we?" I ask, suddenly hugging myself in the flimsy sweater I threw on.

Adrian twists slightly to look at me, his expression serious. "The Baltic Sea, along the German Riviera. Somewhere near Wismar."

I study the name stenciled in ten-foot-high black letters over the hangar doors of a colossal warehouse we're headed toward: TRANSMARINIA.

Of course. Was I supposed to expect their Transylvania references to be subtle? And where else would their Transylvania be, but across the sea instead of the forest?

This is their true Transylvania.

The thought makes my skin go bumpy with a chill. "So, this is where the Shipwright lives," I whisper.

Adrian inclines his head.

But that's not what I really want to know. "And why do you think this builder will help you?"

Adrian and Mrs. Colding glance at each other. "Because the Shipwright is like me."

"And what's that?"

A strange half-smirk twists Adrian's pale lips. "A rulebreaker."

I grin. "My kind of bloodsucker."

As we approach, the warehouse's tall hangar doors yawn open and the *Lair* drifts inside as if into a whale's gullet. I gape. The dock's vastness is astonishing. It soars up for hundreds of feet on either side, its great concrete structure honeycombed with floor upon floor of workshops and walkways. Lights twinkle from the ceiling. A channel of black water splits the dock down the middle, bearing the *Lair* into its depths in eerie procession. It's like the lair of some James Bond villain.

As deckhands toss mooring lines to the workers waiting along the fender-lined channel, a door to the wheelhouse slides back and I jump. I hadn't even noticed Captain Redfearn dip out to man a wing station flybridge with a better overview for docking. He shakes his silver head. "I still think this is too risky," he grumbles.

Adrian claps a hand on his shoulder as he passes. "Duly noted, Arnold." And waiting for the dock's hangar doors to groan closed and block out the ruinous force of the sun, he slips out onto the deck.

We leave the captain to confer with an engineer for a refit of the VIP suite. Within moments, a put-together secretary is leading Adrian, Mrs. Colding and I through the dock into adjoining spaces, her heels clicking smartly on the concrete. I look around in a daze. We pass vast areas devoted to steel cutting, mechanical work, pipe fitting, paint and electrical and carpentry. We pass a prefabrication shop in which craftsmen on scaffolds weld hull plates together in sprays of sparks, a long room in which engineers check the mating of a propeller on its shaft with the use of a blue dye. And it hits me: They've been doing this for a very long time. This tradition extends all the way back to the time of legend.

What strange land have I come to?

"Right through here," the secretary gestures, and takes a seat at a desk outside an office with the words ILSA NACKENKUSSER – DESIGNER stenciled in black on the pebbled glass of a half-open door.

Adrian places a hand on the glass and pushes the door wide.

The Shipwright's office is immaculate, finely appointed. A huge model of a painted yacht hull hangs gleaming from the ceiling while smaller boat models are placed prominently on shelves. Sticky notes cover the far wall beside a blueprint of a work in progress; the other walls are covered in technical drawings charting the evolution of pleasure crafts, dating back from cutting-edge superyachts to yachts to steamships to two-masted schooners in the age of sail.

At the creak of the door, the slender woman bent over a desk covered in drafting papers turns about to unleash an arch smile. *"Guten tag, Herr Voper."*

I can't help it—my jaw hangs. I lean to whisper to Mrs. Colding, "I didn't know there were woman vampires . . ."

"There aren't many of us, I'll grant you," a voice purrs in smoothly accented English. "Though that's by design."

My head jerks. The Shipwright is staring at me with icy aloofness. She must have ears like a fox.

She also has delicate, doll-like features, Aryan-pale and perfect, the blondeness of her long sheet of hair so light it looks silver. Even dressed in a svelte power suit and skirt, she looks no more than eighteen years old. But the bitter sarcasm, the contrived air of cool indifference, is ancient.

Her blue German eyes flick expectantly to Adrian, and he clears his throat. "Ilsa, this is Aurora Strand. My girlfriend."

The Shipwright's pencil-thin eyebrows glide up as she takes my hand in hers. It's firm, and cool, and scarily strong. "Is that so?" She studies me head to toe. "How curious." Looking past me now, she quips, "Mrs. Colding. Still putting up with this old man?"

The chief stewardess sniffs. "When it suits me."

A surprised laugh leaps out of the woman's throat, momentarily banishing centuries of carefully arranged cynicism. "Have I not noticed the trade winds changing, then?"

"Perhaps," Adrian allows stiffly. "And more than you think."

Ilsa Knackenkusser takes us all in, one perfect brow arched on her porcelain doll's face. "Well, well. At last, something exciting." She smirks. "Please. Come in."

SEVEN

When Adrian is done speaking, the Shipwright leans back in her chair behind the cluttered desk, the long fingernails of one hand tapping on blueprints. "That's quite a story, Herr Voper."

Adrian glances at Mrs. Colding and me seated beside him. He's told the Shipwright everything, without evasion or pretense. My coming to the *Lair* and changing him. My plan. Anatoly's demise, and what Anatoly had said. Why we need the name of Volok's boat.

Ilsa Knackenkusser drags her eyes away from where they've wandered off in thought. "So, this was your idea?" She is looking right at me.

I swallow. "Yes."

She absently nods as if, perhaps, she has been impressed. "I must admit, I admire your boldness in telling me, Voper." She leans forward. "You must think I'll be sympathetic to your cause, given my past, yes?" Adrian's jaw flexes. "How do you know I won't tell the yacht club?"

"Because I know you hate them as much as I do."

The Shipwright throws her pretty head back and laughs. Then she shakes it, side to side, in pitying contempt. "You're wrong, Voper," she coos through flawlessly even teeth, and the air leaves the room. Mrs. Colding shoots a look at Adrian. Adrian's eye tics. I feel the blood sizzle in my veins. And then the Shipwright finishes her sentence. "You could never hate them as much as I do."

Relief fights with triumph on Adrian's face. He begins to smile . . . but the Shipwright lifts a smooth palm. "However. I don't know the name of his boat."

All stare. Ilsa shrugs.

"I can only surmise it was bought through a third party to ensure secrecy. The old fiend has grown wary over the years, thinking a challenger will come for his crown."

Adrian shuts his eyes, teeth gritted. A hint of a smile tugs at the Shipwright's lips. "*But.*"

Adrian's eyes crack open.

"I know the boat that belongs to Volok's blood son, Radomir." Adrian glances at me, at Mrs. Colding. "Meaning?"

Ilsa smirks. "Meaning if there's one way to get to Volok, it's through his son."

"Wait a minute, 'blood son'?" I pipe up, feeling like an idiot.

The Shipwright turns her sharp blue eyes on me. "The first person he turned. Our race have a responsibility toward those we turn. It's the closest thing we have to family." Those blues eyes move to Adrian. "As Herr Voper knows all too well."

All turn to Adrian. He shifts in his seat, looking uncomfortable. "I was Volok's other favored blood son, once. Radomir and I . . . we were like brothers, of a sort. We were very close."

"And you will have no qualms hunting him down?" The Shipwright's gaze is piercing.

Adrian swallows, lost in a tangle of old conflicts and regrets, and meets her gaze. "No."

A tension eases in the room. I clear the dryness in my throat. "So how do we find him?"

Ilsa shrugs a delicate shoulder. "That's easy—Radomir's a party animal. You'll find him at the Monaco Yacht Show."

Adrian, Mrs. Colding and I all look at each other, excitement building like a wave. *Maybe this can happen.* Then Adrian stands, buttoning his jacket, and extends a hand. "Thank you, Ilsa."

Her smile is as warm as it can be on that doll-like face. "Anytime." Her eyes slide past him. "I would like a word with Aurora, though, before you leave."

Cold water floods my bowels. Adrian darts an uncertain look at me. "Of course," he says at last, and slips out of the office with an unhappy Mrs. Colding.

Leaving me alone. With a female creature of the night.

She circles her desk and leans back against it, eyeing me with open curiosity. "So, you're the woman who tamed Adrian Voper."

I snort. "I wouldn't go that far."

"Still, that takes some doing." She tilts her head. "Has he told you everything, I wonder?" My heart tightens in my chest. "Such as?"

"Such as why I'm here." She gestures at the vast empire of workshops about us. "Building yachts for the undead."

My throat bobs, and Ilsa takes that as my answer.

"I'm very much like Adrian, in some respects. For instance, after becoming *this*"—she gestures at her unaging, pale self as if at some disease that has overtaken her body—"I decided to kill my maker."

What?

"I wanted to be with my partner," Ilsa clarifies. "But once I was free, the yacht club . . ." Her lips thin. "They found me and turned me again. They also turned my partner in front of my eyes, and threatened to kill him if I ever left Transmarinia."

So that is what happened to make her like this. Bitter and brittle at the edges, prone to sarcastic barbs and sudden, bewildering entreaties for friendship, as was happening now.

"The message was clear," she goes on. "I would never get away. And I've been the exclusive yacht builder for my kind ever since." She steps toward me now, taking my hand in her small, cool ones, her eyes urgent and beseeching and battering my defenses. "And so I would ask yourself, Aurora: Are you ready for this? Is Adrian?"

The ground veers away beneath me, tipping me into anger, into indignant rage cresting like a sun.

"I didn't tell you because—"

"Because *what?*" I glare, hands on hips.

Adrian and I face each other in the master suite. Transmarinia was barely behind us before I dragged him in here, and the room hums with the potential for hurt, for words that will later be regretted.

Adrian sighs and rubs his forehead. "I didn't want to frighten you. Or make you think I was questioning things."

I cross my arms, sullen and vulnerable. "Are you?"

"*No.* But this is serious business—"

"I know. Which is why you should have told me." I huff out a breath, sulkily keeping my distance. Still, my eyes stray to a vase on the nightstand. To the lilies—my favorite—which had replaced all the roses on the *Lair* so beloved by his late wife, and the thought occurs to me: He's gone through so much. The painful relinquishment of his obsessive ways, the need to ritualistically control his life so he could preserve the memory of his wife. How would he not find it difficult, then, to not try to control this mission in order to protect his new love?

An unexpected softness brims up in me, and I take his hands. "We're in this together. We need to make these *decisions* together."

He sighs, nodding. "I'm sorry."

"You need to take *me* seriously."

"I do."

Our foreheads are touching. I shiver in a long breath. "So how do we make sure—"

"Don't worry." He squeezes my hands. "I'll find a way for us to disappear when this is all over."

"But how? How will we avoid what happened to the Shipwright?"

He looks at me, tinged with a rueful gentleness, and wraps me up in his comforting bulk. "I'm working on it."

EIGHT

We arrive in Monaco on the first day of the yacht show.

Monte Carlo is transformed since the last time I saw it. Every berth is full, bristling with sleek boats that are the envy of the world elite, and megayachts too big to moor in Port Hercule crowd the bay. Dozens of white tents, sportscars and milling millionaires dot the quayside, and helicopters zip through the air like a cloud of mosquitoes. The world's biggest superyacht event has begun.

Which means it will be crawling with vampires.

"We're all still in agreement on the plan?" I voice aloud.

Adrian, Captain Redfearn and Mrs. Colding are silent in the wheelhouse, taking in the vista of wealth from behind the *Lair*'s sloping windows. We'd discussed it at length en route. Since Radomir was a party animal, we all knew he'd be in the thick of the show's famous nighttime yacht parties. All Adrian had to do was make a call to get us on the list of the biggest party boat in port, and we were bound to find him.

But would he play ball? The answer, obviously, was that it was too dangerous to risk it, to have things go sideways on another boat surrounded by others of his kind. The only sensible thing to do was to lure him away and onto the *Lair*. Where we could try to make him see reason. (Or get him to talk with the threat of another hull door opening.)

But what could possibly lure an immortal hedonist away from the sparkling offerings of nighttime Monaco?

A piece of ass, of course. What else?

Which meant me.

Me, playing the honeypot again. Me, seducing him.

Adrian had hardly been a fan of this. His lips had snarled back, his shoulders ridging up in anger at the notion. But he'd known it was the only way.

"I'm going with you," he says now as we stare at Monte Carlo.

I nod in agreement, shivering and thinking of not having him at my side, watching me, ensuring my protection on a boat full of nightwalkers.

"I'll have the *Lair* ready to disembark in case we need to make a quick exit," Captain Redfearn proffers.

"Good," I say, my eyes roaming the eateries lining the dock, and add, "I think I'll take a walk along the quai before tonight."

Adrian's shoulders ridge up again. "You think you'll *what?*" Even Mrs. Colding turns in surprise.

"The crews of all the boats will be hanging out in the waterfront bars during the show," I explain. "In order to seduce Radomir, I need to know what he likes in a woman. What his … *tastes* are." I swallow back a tremble in my voice as Adrian scowls and add, dry-mouthed, "Maybe I'll even be able to identify Volok's boat."

Adrian considers it for a moment. But only a moment. "No," he says, jerking his head in dismissal. "I won't allow it—"

"It's daytime. All your kind will be inside their boats. I'll be fine."

"*No.*"

Mrs. Colding glances at Captain Redfearn. "It's a shrewd move, Adrian."

I put a hand on Adrian's arm. "You have to believe in me, remember?"

For a long moment he stands there, teeth clenched and shaking his head. But at last he turns to me. "Be back before dark. I mean it."

I smile at him, threading my arm through his. "I promise."

NINE

Two hours later, with a shiny day pass hanging from my neck, I pass through security and enter the Monaco Yacht Show with my jaw on my chest.

It. Is. *Ridiculous.*

It's like a street market for the one percent. The finest boats in the world line the dock, hulls and nameplates flashing in the sun. Tenders and toys out of a spy film bob in the water or dazzle on display under white tents lining the quai, industry insiders chatting away in exhibitor booths. And if the yachts are the stars at night, the cars are the stars during the day. There are probably more sportscars per square meter here than anywhere else in the world: a fleet of Bugattis and Ferraris and Maseratis, sporty little racing classics and vintage muscle cars. And all of this opulence, of course, is matched by the people who have come to see it. Dressed in my yachtie polo, skirt, and deck shoes, I am wildly out of place amongst the millionaires strolling the quai in the latest Gucci and Armani and Chanel, all of them tanned and healthy and perusing superyachts as if shopping for a new bike. I feel like a child who's wandered into a fabulous ball reserved only for adults.

But I haven't come here to dance. I turn to study the row of stern-docked yachts, and it's not hard—not hard at all—to identify what I'm looking for.

They spread out before me, rippling from the stern flagstaffs of one boat after another, up into the dozens—that yacht club burgee with its sigil of geometric fangs.

They're everywhere.

Chills sweep me head to toe. I force myself to look down, look away. Now to check the nameplates. They far from dispel the suspiciousness of the burgees: *Sepulcher*, *Blood Vessel*, *Demon Bride*.

Not exactly subtle, guys.

When I find her, she's right in front of me: *Neck Romancer.*

I suppress an eye roll. What was I expecting, though? What else would an undead hellraiser like Radomir name his yacht?

I take a moment to study it. She's not big, but sleek, ultra-luxurious, and predatory in an almost sexy way, with a gleaming silver shell that turns into a flashy red at the stern, its articulated aft stairs dipped in popping scarlet. Her lights are off, no crew to be seen. She's also not taking any tours during the show. A sign hanging at the end of her passerelle reads "Private Yacht—No Boarding."

It's hard not to think of what is lurking on that boat. And what goes on inside, behind the privacy of those tinted windows.

I shiver.

Spotting a deckhand wiping down a rail with a chamois on the next boat over, I ask after the favorite haunt of the superyacht crews. A finger points across the port at a restaurant that looks like an upscale warehouse. "You'll find 'em at Stars 'N' Bars."

A sports bar, as it turns out. A sprawling, three-level American-style diner with checkered tiles and red-leather booths, strangely jarring amidst Monaco's European elegance. It's also crammed with sports memorabilia. Crowded walls of fame, Olympic bobsleighs and Terry boots, glass-encased motor racer suits and even a full-sized Formula 1 racecar hanging nose-down on a wall. One glance at the patrons glued to the dozens of TV screens everywhere tells me the bar caters to the expat community, but I don't see any yachties yet. So I head upstairs.

At the top step I freeze, looking about at the open-air lounge bar with its breathtaking views of the harbor and skyline. It's filled with the white polos of yachties, crew passes hanging from tanned necks.

Very slowly, I tuck my visitor's pass into my pocket and belly up to the bar.

I order a gin and tonic—because I need a tonic right now. With the cool glass gripped tight in my hand, I summon up all my nerves and approach a table crowded with a rambunctious lot with Australian and South African accents. "Mind if I join?" I say, gesturing. "I got off early and . . ."

"Yeah, yeah, yeah," waves a cheery-faced bosun, and everyone makes room for me to slip into the booth. "Which boat you working, love?" They all glance at my chest where my crew pass should be, and I flail about in my memory. "Oh. The, uh, *Sepulcher?*"

"Nice," a blonde stewardess says with breathy enthusiasm. "That's a good boat."

"Yeah, definitely." I try to make it as casual as possible. "You know, I'm always up for new experiences, though."

The yachties exchange knowing looks. "You wanting to try a new boat?"

"Welllll . . ." I say, shrugging, and they all laugh. "You know. *Maaaaybe.* I hear the *Neck Romancer* is a good boat to work on . . ."

More exchanged looks. These ones different. "Where'd you hear that?"

I almost choke on a sip of gin. "What do you mean?"

The bosun shrugs. "Just, you know. You hear things." He juts his chin. "You wanna try, though, knock yourself out. Her crew is right over there."

I turn to look—a private table of crew members in all-black uniforms, huddled over drinks. They look miserable.

"They like to keep to themselves," comes the breathy whisper in my ear. "A bunch of cold fish, if you ask me."

As I watch, a thin stewardess gets up to approach the bar.

"Ehhhh!"

I startle. The crew at my table lean back to welcome the arrival of burgers and fries. I take the opportunity to flash a smile and dip away.

I reach the bar seconds after the stewardess from the *Neck Romancer*. She's waiting on another round of drinks, shifting from foot to foot. She raises a tentative hand. "And remember—no cinnamon for garnish!" she calls, adding in a small, meek voice, "I'm, like, *super* allergic."

I lift my glass for the bartender to see and set it on the bartop, glancing at the stewardess. She's even skinnier than I thought, almost anemic-looking, with a jumpy mousiness I know all too well. She keeps pulling at a strand of dark hair.

"The *Neck Romancer*, huh?"

She jerks at my voice. "What?" Then, glancing at her crew pass, "Oh, yeah." Not exactly brimming over with enthusiasm.

"The *Sepulcher*," I announce, gesturing at my chest. "Sorry, my pass is back at my table. Name's Alexis."

"Riley," murmurs the girl. Her smile is polite, tight-lipped.

"So," I ask, indicating her pass again. "What's it like working there?" Going off the speed of the bartender, I probably have another minute before this stewardess returns to her table. And the sun, I realize with a sudden constricting of my stomach, is far lower in the sky than I'd like it to be.

"Oh, I . . ." Riley's face breaks out in a series of tics, and she tugs again at her hair. "I signed a non-disclosure agreement . . ."

"Totally. Got it." The bartender sets aside drink two. One more to go. "You can tell me a little bit about Radomir, though, yeah?" I flash an encouraging grin. "I hear he's quite the ladies' man . . ."

But her eyes round at the invocation of his name. She glances at her table—her crewmates are watching us. "I . . ."

"What, he hasn't taken an interest in you?"

At this, Riley sputters out a laugh. "No, he wouldn't." Her hand works in her hair. Twisting. Pulling. Jerks suddenly away from her head. "He likes his girls . . . more forward."

There are long dark strands clenched between her fingers. And it's now that I notice, under the careful arrangement of plaits, the white gleam of scalp.

An impulse disorder.

My flesh creeps and I think, *This girl is terrified out of her wits.*

A man at Riley's table rises, eyes locked on us. But Riley hasn't noticed yet.

I shift forward, keeping the stew's gaze on me as her last cocktail is placed on the bartop. "So, what kind of girl would I have to be, to get hired? Or, say"—I shrug a shoulder—"get his attention?"

But Riley gulps, as if this were an appalling thought. "I dunno. I mean . . . there's a lot of turnover. Especially since we also work on Volok's boat."

My gut tumbles, and I'm barely aware that the sun is dipping alarmingly behind the steep hillside of Monaco. "Volok?" I echo. "The crew of Radomir's boat also work on his father's?"

The man at Riley's table starts toward us. Riley seeing stiffens, grabs at her drinks. "I . . . I shouldn't have said that. I gotta go." She scurries past, and by the time the bartender turns to offer my cocktail I'm not there. By the time the man from the *Neck Romancer* turns from a head-hung Riley to scan the lounge I'm nowhere to be seen, down the stairs, hurrying back to the *Lair* in the darkening port with a thrilling lightness in my chest.

TEN

Full night has descended on Monaco by the time Captain Redfearn taxis me back to the *Lair*. I expect to see Adrian pacing back and forth on the swim deck, packs of muscle clenched in anger, but that's not who's waiting for me.

"Where is he?" I ask as the limo tender drifts close, and Mrs. Colding clasps her hands before her and purses her lips.

"The observation lounge."

Anxiety pushes up into my throat. I'm a mess of nerves as I find the library and slip through its hidden door in the bookcase, full of regret and a small, indignant exasperation. But I can't be distracted. I have to concentrate on my feet. Next, it's the white-painted stairs behind the door, conducting down into darkness. And then the long corridor leading into the enormous space of the underwater observation lounge, cold and clean and alive with refracted light wavering on the walls.

Adrian stands before the immense expanse of glass set into the hull, studying his reflection. He is very still, one hand in a trouser pocket, his hair dark and glossy in the play of light down

here. Near the top of the glass above him, the waterline dances. And above that, very distant, the palace of Monaco, an exquisite tiara of light.

The sight of Adrian there makes me think of the first time I saw him in this room. Back before he was Adrian to me—before there was us—and there was only a scared stewardess and a billionaire who did not know how to tell the girl he liked what he was. A wave of tenderness rolls through me, loosening my throat. And then I remember why I'm here.

"I know I said I'd be back before nightfall," I say softly, the words echoing in that space as I step closer. "And I was. There was still light out when I left, I wasn't in any—" I shut my eyes, swallowing down a rising resentment. *You don't have to apologize or defend yourself.* "And it worked. I talked to a stewardess on Radomir's boat. He likes women who take charge."

But he doesn't say anything. He doesn't turn. His head is bowed, as if in disgust. Or anger. *I'll give you anger, then.* "Why don't you believe in me?" I snap, shoulders heaving. "If you'd just give me a chance—"

"I do believe in you, Aurora," he says at last, and turns about. "I believe in us."

I see now he wasn't studying his reflection. He has an iPad in his hand and is holding it out to me.

I give him a cagey glare and take it. It shows an ad for some stately old mansion tucked away in the Colorado mountains, like some less-creepy twin of that hotel in that one Stephen King classic.

"What's this?" I sigh.

"It's where we're going," he says, a slow grin hitching up one side of his mouth. "When we're done with this."

"What do you mean?"

"It's for us," he explains. "I just bought it."

The room quivers. "You serious?"

His smile is blinding now, filling all of that dark cave with its brilliance. "It's our way out. I'll give up yachting, and we'll go inland. It's the last place my kind would want to go. And I figure the mountains of Colorado are as inland as you can get."

"But . . . what about the *Lair*?"

"I'm done with that life, Arie. *You're* my life now."

You're my life.

My blood sings. The breath goes from my lungs. Sudden, blinding need rockets up out of me.

So, Mrs. Colding was right.

I let the iPad clatter to the floor—Adrian's eyebrows go up—and before I know it I've grabbed him by his shirt and thunked him back against the observation window, my lips pressed hard against his. After a long moment he pulls back, a bit out of breath.

"You sure?"

I grunt impatiently, biting my lip. "Mm-hmm."

"Really sure?"

I grab him by the scruff of his neck. "Just fuck me already."

He stills, a ravening hunger hazing his vivid blue eyes. A muscle twitches in his sharp jaw.

Then we snap.

We both fumble at our clothes. I lift my polo over my head and unclasp my bra, and he groans deep in his throat as my breasts bounce free. Then he's groping at his belt buckle and I'm unbuttoning his shirt with clumsy, trembling hands, aching to feel his bare flesh against mine. I feel like a teenager again.

Apparently, I take too long—he growls in impatience and rips his shirt wide, sending the last few buttons skittering across the floor, and I hurriedly shimmy the shirt off him. Then he's yanked my yachtie skirt down and wrenched my panties to the side, one of my legs wrapped around him as he thrusts inside, bumping me hard against the observation window. I gasp and claw at his shoulders, goose bumps breaking out all over me at the coldness of the glass—and his fullness. *Jesus*, I'd forgotten how big he feels. How *good* he feels. His mouth seals mine, sucking hungrily at my bottom lip, and I moan into his mouth. I hold his face, and our eyes find each other. *God, I missed this. I missed us, Adrian.*

I'm trembling all over as he begins to make love to me.

I pull him close; I can't pull him close enough. I arch and press my breasts into his chest as we kiss each other, achingly slowly. I do not know for the longest time that tears are running out of the corners of my eyes. I laugh, we both laugh, like children amazed at wonders they do not understand. This moment—the hope for this moment—had been like something I could never dare look at directly, for fear of it vanishing. It was a stab of light.

But it is here now. It is here.

Adrian's teeth nip at my ear, and I shiver. His skin under my hands—the muscles in his shoulders bunching like wings—makes me melt. He cups my ass and firmly squeezes as he grinds into me, the dense wall of his abs pressed hard against my tummy. The closeness, the exquisite steamy intimacy of the movement, takes my breath away. Perhaps it's the proof of it that excites me—the proof of his passion. Josh, after all, had never shown his. We were like two solid worlds trying to become one. He would try and try, as if with his sudden, penetrating violence he could enter my world. But he never did. Nothing ever gave way.

But isn't that what sex is? A violent act, a flash of insanity, a claim of possession brutal as lightning. A wicked breakthrough in a proper world. As long as—and this was key—the woman wanted to be engulfed in the insanity of that man.

How strange. The violence that's welcome, and the violence that's not.

Let's see if I'm ready for it.

I pull away—Adrian stares—and I turn about to press my hands, my breasts, my cheek to the hard glass of the observation window. Offering my ass.

But Adrian hesitates, knowing we've never been in this position before, with him behind and me totally defenseless against him. He looks for consent in my look—the word *gentleman* flashes through my mind—and I reach back for him, swollen lips parted. *Please*.

So he obliges.

New pounding and sundering pleasures. My nipples perked and rubbing hard against the cool glass. It's a shivery, almost out-of-body thrill to be taken against that immense windowpane looking out on the deeps—to be ravaged, reduced, exhausted. And to be the one inviting it. I arch my ass against it, a bounty of flesh for him, feeling newly and boundlessly resourceful, flushed with power. And he takes it. He begins to pound harder and harder, making my ass cheeks bounce. The loud slapping noises and desperate declarations filling that dark, cavernous space. *(Yes. Yes, baby. Please.)* Adrian's firm hands gripping my hips, his thumbs in the dimples at the base of my spine. My rampant hair falling about my face. He snarls in his need and fists a hand in that hair, yanks with savage force so that my head is thrown back and my throat is bared like an animal's. I moan, deep and luxurious, as someone waking from a dream. As someone waking, at long last, from fear.

And behind me, in the glass, Adrian's pale reflection. Tender and vulnerable in its ecstasy close to torment.

I wait and wait. But the reflection does not change, does not reveal a sinister new face.

It remains, unbetrayingly, only Adrian.

As if I am hovering. I am hovering now in my happiness. The feeling spirals up and up, swelling my lungs, my throat, pressing behind my eyes. A stab of light.

Before me in that calm and silent world beyond the glass, fish dart by, glimmering and free.

ELEVEN

Later on the top deck Adrian, Mrs. Colding, Captain Redfearn and I all drink cocktails as we wait for the yacht parties to start, the benighted port beyond a dazzling lightshow. I glow with contentment. Adrian has curled himself onto the same sun lounger with me, wrapping me in his arms in the easy, unabashed way of a teenager, and I don't think I could be any happier. Mrs. Colding glances at me, a knowing flicker of a smile at the corner of her mouth, before turning back to the nocturnal glamour of Monaco.

"How long do we have?" she asks.

Adrian checks his watch. "Another three hours. The yacht parties get started late."

"Then you all have plenty of time," Captain Redfearn grunts, pouring a drink for Mrs. Colding, "to get a good buzz on."

We all look at each other, repressed smiles dimpling our cheeks, and Mrs. Colding snorts. She sounds positively girlish.

"Aye, aye, captain," I salute, gulping back my margarita. Adrian smiles and tucks a lock of hair behind my ear, making me shiver. It's hard to look at him, I have to lay my head on his shoulder. I'm almost too happy to believe this new change in him.

It has its effect on the others, too. After a while Captain Redfearn rouses from his thoughts. "It's been a while, hasn't it?"

Adrian turns to him.

"Since that night you hired me."

Adrian returns his gaze to the cliffs of Monaco. "It has."

"He never told you the story, did he?" The captain, addressing me now.

I shake my head. Mrs. Colding is listening attentively—clearly, she's never heard this story, either.

But Adrian protests. "Arnold, you don't have to—"

"No, I want to tell them." A steely look, a rare hardness of the voice which Adrian acquiesces to, lifting a hand.

All right.

Captain Redfearn inclines his head in a stern, grateful nod and begins. "This was some time ago. I was a little rougher then. Divorced. Hadn't seen my daughter in years. We'd had a falling out, my anger . . ." He shakes his head. "But I'd had success with yachting, made a decent living. I'd just ended a charter in St. Barthes when I got the call." His throat bobs. "It was my daughter. She'd gone missing. Went to volunteer in a third world country and never returned. My wife . . . she thought it was my fault. That I'd estranged her. Made her want nothing to do with us." He glances at our drinks with a pained smile on his face, and it dawns on me now that he doesn't have a cocktail of his own. "I didn't take it well. I turned to gambling and drink. Burned a lot of bridges. Got to a point where it was pretty clear I was nearing the end of my rope in this industry. And one night, I was up there"—he points at the Casino de Monte Carlo glittering on the cliffs above—"when some friends decided to collect on their debt. I marched straight out the front doors as if I hadn't a care in the world, and when the men followed me, shouting, it was exactly what I wanted. Something terrible surged through me, like a whale gliding underwater, and I whirled on them, and . . ." He looks up, a different smile on his face now. "And there you were, Mr. Voper. Standing between us as if you'd flowed out of the night. And maybe . . . maybe it was the potential for violence I saw in you that made me stop. Maybe it was that." Adrian looks down, jaw muscles cording in his pale cheeks. "And I knew. I knew that whatever anger I had, it was nothing compared to . . ." The captain looks away suddenly, slides one rough palm against the other. "Anyway. He paid my debt, all eighty grand. Wrote a check on the goddamn spot. Helped me kick my gambling and drinking. And then he asked me to skipper the *Lair*. And that"—he sucks in a long, shaky breath—"was that, as they say." He pours himself a glass of soda water and lifts it. "And that is why I follow you, Adrian Voper."

Mrs. Colding's eyes are shining. She lifts her glass, too.

I lift mine, heart thundering, and turn to look up into Adrian's face. A solemness has draped itself on him like a cloak. He looks out at us, eyes bright, like a man invited into a home after a long, dark stretch on the road.

"Thank you," he says, and his voice trembles.

My Adrian, I think. *This is my Adrian.*

It's all around me now. The glow of being singled out, so unexpectedly chosen by such a man. Being with such a man. I snuggle close, burrowing into his arms, and listen to Mrs. Colding and Captain Redfearn swap yachting stories. It's hard not to snort with laughter. They're full of ridiculous standards and outrageous requests, as shallow and scandalous as a reality TV show. Before long I'm hearing about having to chopper in blueberries from a small hometown in Russia for breakfast the next morning. Being ordered to hose salt off the boat during a hurricane. The wives of guests cornering you in the bridge at night to give you a blowjob. They're like the stories one tells about melodramatic marriages, in wonder at the wicked childishness of it all. What can you do but laugh? And as I watch Mrs. Colding sit there with her glass held primly in her lap, eyes shut as she listens to Captain Redfearn gamely take up the next tale with the gruff brevity and dry wit of a seasoned sailor, I know that this honor I'm feeling, this flare-up of pride, extends further. For this captain and chief stewardess—they're not here just for Adrian. They're here for me, too. What we're doing together. It's only been a few months—a few strange, dreamlike months—and I've shared with these people my hopes and fears, and cried in front of them, and had my heart broken with them, and despite me upending their lives to plunge them into my mad plan to free Adrian, they have stuck it out. Because that is what family does—fight for each other.

Their stories go on and on, floating on the warm air of Monaco, wrapping me in a soft, sweet glow that lets me know, deep in my bones, I have never felt so safe. And this is how I doze off—with my cheek on Adrian's shoulder and his hand playing through my hair, listening to what my family is saying.

TWELVE

It's ten o'clock when Adrian and I set out for the yacht party.

I've dressed to kill: a knockout black dress with a plunging neckline, astronomical heels that show off my calves, my hair curled to the side in a soft, glamorous wave and a slash of red lipstick that screams sex. Adrian has gone suitably nautical: double-breasted navy blazer, lightweight shirt, white chinos, bare feet in blue suede boat shoes. He takes in my look as I try not to twist my ankles on Monaco's cobblestones. "Subtle."

"Yeah, well," I wheeze, holding onto him for balance, "I have a feeling subtlety isn't Radomir's thing."

Adrian grunts, eyeing my cleavage. "Did you have to give him *that* much to look at, though?"

"You two done arguing yet?" Mrs. Colding crackles in my ear.

I grimace and reach up to adjust my earpiece. All four of us are wearing them, to keep in contact throughout the night. Captain Redfearn waiting back at the *Lair*, Mrs. Colding across the street from the quai with a pair of high-powered binoculars to watch both the *Neck*

Romancer and the party boats. "Doubt it," I respond, giving Adrian a smirk.

Mrs. Colding ignores me. "Remember, you two shouldn't be seen together. So separate as soon as you board. We don't want Arie being associated with Adrian and identified."

"Roger that."

We're on the blue carpet rolled out on the docks now, passing the sterns of yachts glowing with clublike lighting, lines of flags from around the world strung from their poles. All of Monaco is here. The fashionable rich drift on and off boats, hopping from yacht to yacht, party to party. Among them, somewhere, Radomir. And among all of them, everywhere, Adrian's kind.

My flesh is prickled with goose bumps by the time we arrive at our destination: the *Crypt,* a gleaming three-hundred-foot superyacht thumping with music, laughter and the buzz of conversation drifting out over the water. The center of the yacht show after-party.

There's a pavilion at the foot of the passerelle. It's populated by burly men in suits and a deceivingly cheerful hostess—the security check. Adrian gives his name and mine (my handy alias, Alexis Hobbs), and they check our ID. A moment of rubber-legged dread as they study my forged one. Then we're through, leaving our shoes in a basket along with all the other footwear of the super-rich, because we can't scuff that teak, can we?

Seems we've pulled off the first step, and I'll only be remembered tonight as some mysterious plus one whose name won't be found anywhere but on that hostess' list.

Even so, I slow on the passerelle. I suddenly feel as if my arms, my legs, my stomach have been filled with cement. I put out a hand on the rail and take in a long, steadying breath through puckered lips, my eyes on the blurs of figures crowding the yacht. It's one thing to lure a man back to the *Lair*. But one of *them* . . .

What am I doing? Have I gone crazy?

Adrian follows my gaze and touches the small of my back, the contact spreading—warm and reassuring—up my spine. "Don't worry. I'll be watching you every second."

I give him a dirty look. "I *know* you will." But my façade crumbles almost immediately. My lip trembles, my eyes wide as they stare into his. He grips my hand tight.

"Hey. I won't let anything happen to you, okay? I promise."

I nod, swallowing a lump in my throat. "Okay." Whipping my hair out of my face: "Okay."

"Good luck, Arie." Mrs. Colding and Captain Redfearn.

"Thanks." And lifting my chin and leveling my eyes, I stalk onto the boat, separating from Adrian at the head of the passerelle.

I'm on my own.

It's quite the cocktail party in dockside Monaco. A five-piece band strolls about the boat playing cool jazz, and the DJ pumps out upbeat pop and techno music from the top deck. Statuesque hostesses drift about with trays of caviar or oversized bottles of rosé and champagne. I grab a glass and sip back a bracing mouthful of bubbly, scanning the boat. Every person crowding it is clothed in a casual, almost carelessly advertised wealth. The men with incredible timepieces, the women with jewels winking at ear and bosom, heads bent in delicious gossip.

"Well, the wife, she came back early from her shopping ashore, checking for pubic hairs in the beds, so I didn't have time to chopper the hookers off the boat." Peals of laughter. "Had my chief stew hide them in her quarters for two days."

I move on to a circle of media magnates.

"You wouldn't believe the things I pay for. Just last week, a new deckhand had a miscommunication with the fuel guy when we were in port in Barcelona. Said 'petrol' instead of 'Super 95.' So, guess what this Spaniard did?" Groans. "Yep. Filled the boat with diesel instead of petroleum. Had to have all the fuel tanks pumped and cleaned out. Fucking mess."

And technology tycoons.

"Russians? Don't get me started. I mean, how do you manage to get shit on a bathroom ceiling?"

The intimacy of the conversations makes it clear. These people, the wealthiest in the world, all know each other. It's a small club, after all. And so someone like me—someone unknown—is a novelty, to be treated with curiosity if not distrust. Heads turn and eyes crawl over me, sizing me up, and I wonder which of them have no hearts pumping in their chests, no blood moving in their veins. Heartless capitalists personified.

The Wet Set, indeed.

How philosophical I get when I am hovering in the airy space of terror.

I look about but can't find Adrian anywhere. He has melted into the crowd. "You still with me?" I whisper.

"Always," he purrs into my ear, and I spot him now, hands in pockets, standing at the end of the portside gangway. He angles his head at the decks above. "If he's here, Radomir will be in the thick of the party, so you may want to check the pool situation."

I hear a splash above me, shrieks of laughter. Of course.

It's quite the scene. Dancing is general, bodies surging up and down to the beat. Pretty young things splash in the lit-up pool with exaggerated squeals of delight, bikinis or party dresses clinging to every sultry curve. Men flock around them like predators around a watering hole, leaning down to pour bubbly into their open mouths to the cheers of their fellows. I scowl even as something stirs in me, a remote excitement.

"Looking for someone?"

I jump. Some twentysomething tycoon heir with the preppy good looks of an Abercrombie & Fitch model. Already over it. "Not really."

The guy smirks, his eyes dropping to my chest. "You look like you're looking for someone."

"I wouldn't mind eating this guy," Adrian growls in my ear.

"Okay. Later then." I disengage as Mr. Inheritance looks flabbergasted. He's probably had no one turn down his checkbook in his life.

But I'm busy. Because I've seen, up on the sun deck, something I don't like.

One of the hostesses has been cornered up there by a paunchy businessman in an ill-fitting suit. She clutches one of the giant champagne bottles to her chest and tugs an arm away from a grubby, overfamiliar hand as I approach. "No. Please. I'm flattered, but—"

Another hand slides down her back to her ass as he presses close, sweaty lips puckering toward her cringing face. "Aren't you supposed to make the guests hap—*fuck!*"

He grimaces as I crush his wandering hand in a death grip and whip it back. Veins stand out on his flushing brow as I lean in. "No means no, asshole. Understand?"

"Jesus fuck, get the fuck off—"

"*Understand?*" I grit between clenched teeth, squeezing harder, and the man whimpers. "Fucking Christ, all right!"

I let go, blinking and dazed as if emerging from some demon-possessed state, and the man hurries away, glaring at me as he cradles his hand.

The hostess eyes me openmouthed.

"You okay?" I ask.

She jerks her head in a nod, eyes glassy. Then lunges forward and touches my arm. "Thank you," she whispers and dips past for the stairs and the safety of the party.

I'm trembling, my body just now catching up to what I did. The reality of what I did. I reach out to steady myself on a handrail, sucking in huge gulps of air. And here it comes, the throat-tightening cascade of relief mixed with terror one feels after narrowly avoiding a terrible accident. *That could have happened. That could have been bad.*

How close terror is, I wonder, to the burning thrill of pride and triumph.

"That sounded entertaining." Adrian's voice startles me—I'd almost forgotten he was in my ear. "I wish I could've been there to see it."

I snort, swiping my hair away from my face with a shaky hand. "Is that so?"

"Damn right."

I fight back a smile, feeling a flush creeping up my neck. *How can his voice still do this to me?* "Well, maybe you should come up here then, and we can turn these earpieces off for a little while."

"Guys . . ." Captain Redfearn warns.

But I can hear the grin in Adrian's voice. "Just tell me where you are. I lost you when you dashed off."

"Oh, I'm up here on the—"

"He's here," interjects Mrs. Colding's voice. It is low and tight with anxiety. "Radomir is here. He's boarding the boat now."

I lurch to the rail, looking back toward the quai. Mrs. Colding is across the street, slashing her arm and pointing. I follow her directions, looking out over the *Crypt*. The top deck with its pool party, the milling gossipers on the main deck. "Where?"

But then I see him. It has to be him. I spot the two brutish thugs in dark suits first, forging a path to the pool party. And between them, surprisingly short, a leanly muscled party boy in a showy red leather jacket, his blond hair gleaming from here.

"I got him. Adrian, meet me at the pool bar?" I wait, but there's only the crackle of silence. "Adrian?" I wince as my earpiece gives off a static whine and try to adjust it. "Hello?" I grit my teeth. "I think I lost Adrian."

"Sit tight. Just wait at the bar for him," Mrs. Colding warns.

I shake my head. "I can't lose him." I look down again to see Radomir greeted by a horde of revelers and sigh. "Fuck it. I'm going after him."

"Arie, don't—"

I whirl for the stairs and stop with my heart in my throat.

The sun deck. I'd thought it was deserted. An unlit stretch of loungers and whirlpools and canopies fluttering forlornly in the dark. But the dark is not still. A dainty figure in a boldly tailored suit flows out of it. The suit has an Italian cut, the man inside it Italian features, gray and cadaverous-looking. As I watch, he removes a handkerchief from his suit and dabs at the corner of his mouth, tucks it away again.

Signore Spalatro tilts his head and smiles a toothsome smile. "Ciao, Signorina Strand."

THIRTEEN

It takes me what feels like forever to form a reply. I have to speak past the sudden dryness in my throat. "Signore Spalatro. What a surprise."

"Oh no," Mrs. Colding says in my ear, in a sinking tone.

Spalatro. Anatoly's friend, who visited the *Lair* only weeks ago. And who now must be wondering where his friend went.

It's in moments like these that you clasp your hands together, like Mrs. Colding, to hide that they are shaking.

"Indeed. A curious surprise," Spalatro remarks, stepping closer. Each step is a jump in my heartrate. The din of the party has faded away. My entire world hangs on every word emitted from those dainty, colorless lips. "Who would have thought I would find you here?" His opaque eyes go past me. "Accompanying Mr. Voper, are you?"

"Say you're not," Mrs. Colding crackles.

"No," I blurt, so fast it's almost a hiccup. "No. I'm done with him. Trying out other prospects."

The bloodless lips curve up. "I see. That kind of girl, eh?"

"Yeah," I breathe, swaying back and forth on that deck. "That kind of girl."

"So you wouldn't know anything then about Anatoly's disappearance?"

My stomach drops. "Disappearance?" I say as innocently as I can.

"Shit," Captain Redfearn says in my ear.

The cold eyes narrow. "He hasn't been seen for a few weeks now. It's the strangest thing—the last I heard from him he was on his way to visit Mr. Voper." He is very close now. I can see the pinched skin at the corners of his mouth, faintly ruddy as if stained, over the years, from countless feedings. There is something ferretlike and diseased about it. Obscene. "Now isn't that strange?"

I glance back down at the pool party, where Radomir is engulfed in a parade of women. "Well, it was swell catching up. Gotta go."

And I brush past him, shoulders hunched and breath held, as if afraid of inhaling some pestilence. A sob fights to get out of my throat.

That's when I see the Jacuzzi on the sun deck is not empty. There's a log floating in it, a huge champagne bottle beside it. But I know that's no log.

The hostess is faceup, eyes wet and open, her expression that of someone puzzling through some mystifying development. Blood flows out of the two delicate holes in her neck and curls like a pinkish plague into the water about her.

So. I couldn't save her after all.

"It's very easy for people to disappear in this world, no?" Spalatro, at my shoulder, in an evil, loving whisper. The nape of my neck crawls. My lashes bat away a tear forming in the corner of one eye.

"Get away," Mrs. Colding crackles. "Move. *Now*."

"I think," I say in a soft and cracking voice, "I think you've got me mixed up with—"

"Oh, but you *are* mixed up in this, signorina," Spalatro says, his hands gliding about my shoulders like a lover. "You see, I heard a rumor. A rumor about a young woman. Beautiful. Dark-haired." A long, pale, taloned hand brushes at my hair, making me flinch. "She was in a yachtie bar today, asking after Radomir." My heart constricts. "She claimed she was from the *Sepulcher*, but she wasn't. Because no girl called Alexis works on that boat. Now why would she lie about that?" I keep very still, not daring to breathe. Spalatro feigns pontification. "And then I think, Anatoly. And I think, Will what happened to him happen to Radomir? To the Commodore?"

I shut my eyes.

I can hear it in his voice. That stained mouth smiling in triumph. "So, my lovely one. Are you going to tell me what happened to my friend?"

"Where the hell are you, Adrian?" Mrs. Colding's voice, for the first time, has become shrill.

"Because if you don't," Spalatro continues, "I'm going to make sure Adrian never leaves this boat. And you'll be watching when I dismember him with a hacksaw and feed him to the sharks."

A cold, vengeful rage seeps into my gut. Mrs. Colding somehow senses it. "Don't. Say. Anything," she warns.

"Sure," I whisper, because I can't stop myself. Because I know now that I'm not getting out of this.

Death or undeath awaits me, and all I can do is put it off for a few moments longer.

"You want to know what happened?" I ask. Spalatro gives his ear, and I whisper into it with delicious relish. "I gave him a tan."

The vampire's pale face slackens.

A beastly snarl schisms the night and I'm suddenly flung to the teak deck, Spalatro looming over me. Something is happening to that stained mouth. His fangs are lengthening, protruding out from behind his upper lip and gnashing into the bottom one in his fury. He does not seem to notice. Blood pitter-patters onto the deck.

"Adrian," I pray under my breath, full of panic. "Help me."

The thing that was once Spalatro cocks its head. "What's that?"

I hold my breath.

But the thing smiles. "Oh, this will be fun," it says, and lunges for me.

The decision strikes me like lightning. I snatch the neck of the oversized champagne bottle bobbing in the Jacuzzi and swing blindly. It connects with a hollow *donk* with Spalatro's head. He grunts and falls to one knee, hand held to scalp, as he blinks in awful confusion at the deck. I scramble back and wait—for what, I don't know—clutching my stomach and tasting the telltale nastiness of vomit rising in my throat. And then the flap of skin peels away from Spalatro's scalp, sending blood sheeting down his face, and he holds up his hands and shrieks.

The world stutters. Spalatro crawls to me. A hand grips my bare leg, freezing to the touch, another presses down on my hip, pinning me to the Jacuzzi's wooden steps, and Spalatro hauls himself up my body. I slap at him, thinking, *I should scream. This is when I should scream.* But I can't. It's lodged somewhere far down inside me, somewhere I can never free it from. Mrs. Colding and Captain Redfearn are shouting in my ear, but I cannot hear them. All I can hear is Spalatro's slavering breath, cold and fetid on my face. It smells of blood and rotten flesh. Carrion meat. It smells of death. Then his hands are about my throat, the blood filling one of his eye sockets, glazing the eyeball crimson and beading his lashes, dripping onto my face. And he peels his stained lips back from his long, white fangs like a coroner opening a corpse. *How is this happening?* my mind gibbers. *What is happening? I am at a party on a superyacht in glamorous Monaco, and a man that is not a man is about to suck my blood. What is—*

That is when a pair of pale hands grip Spalatro's head and wrenches it off his shoulders with a loud *plop*.

I blink. Adrian stands above me, chest heaving and white chinos soaked in blood, holding Spalatro's dripping head by the hair in one hand. Our eyes lock.

Then there's a high, shrill, bloodcurdling scream. It's not mine—that scream never made it out.

No. Someone is screaming below, down by the pool on the main deck, in the normal world. Screaming and pointing up at Adrian revealed in the sudden spotlight of the party's attention.

The yacht falls silent. The music stops.

Adrian and I look at each other. "Go," he says.

I start to rise. "But—"

"*Go*," he growls, Spalatro's head thudding to the deck, and before I can stop him he dashes to the rail and leaps into the night.

"Oh my God," Mrs. Colding breathes in my ear.

I scramble up. Adrian arcs, impossibly far, onto the neighboring yacht, landing with a crash on the main deck gangway. I know I should run, flee this crime scene and get back to the *Lair*. But I can't. I am rooted to the spot, the hairs on my arms standing straight up, unable to peel my eyes away. Because Adrian is not alone. There is a pounding of feet and other shapes follow him through the air from the *Crypt*, men in Eurotrash nightclub-crawler outfits. Adrian turns one way, then the other, but a door slides back and more shapes glide out onto the gangway.

He is hemmed in on either side. Nowhere to go. Trapped.

"No," I whisper.

He looks at me then, across the span between the two boats. His eyes piercing my heart. His voice, crackling to life in my ear, is soft as velvet. "You'll always be my Northern Light, Aurora." And he takes out his earpiece and tosses it over the side as the shapes grab him.

That is when I scream.

FOURTEEN

I feel heavy and sluggish as Mrs. Colding hustles me away from the *Crypt*, as if a sack has been dumped over my head. The other fleeing partiers darting past keep throwing scandalized looks my way, white and squinting in the strobing glare of the police lights, but Mrs. Colding ignores them all. She doesn't say a word at first. She keeps wiping at my face. The blood.

"Are you okay, dear?"

"He jumped so far."

She nods, concentrating on her work. "He did."

"It all went so wrong."

She stops to peer intently into my face. I look down at my feet bleeding on the cobblestones. "We forgot my shoes."

"Yes," Mrs. Colding says slowly, and tugs my hand. "Come on. We need to go."

She keeps looking at me in the stern of the tender boat as Captain Redfearn motors us back to the *Lair*. They exchange a look.

"Arie?"

"Mmm?"

"You weren't hurt. Do you understand? You weren't bitten."

"Oh," I say, nodding my head. "That's good." After a moment I add, my eyes on the *Crypt*, "They must have deep pockets to cover up something like that."

Another exchanged look. Mrs. Colding scootches closer and holds my hand, trying to connect me back to reality. "It's okay if you want to cry."

"No, I'm okay. Thanks, Mrs. Colding."

"Okay."

I sit there and hold her hand, the tears streaming out of the corners of my eyes, back across my temples, into my hair blowing in the wind.

Later, we gather around the long dining table in the *Lair*. Captain Redfearn stands, rough hands on the smooth wood, head down. Mrs. Colding keeps blinking rapidly and looking away. I do not move. I stare resolutely at the head of the table. At the empty chair where Adrian would sit. Where he did sit when we had our meeting that would decide our relationship. But as much as I try, I cannot will him there. I cannot see that achingly familiar figure, that one astonishingly compact, reserved and haunted package, which has somehow become the sole arbiter of my happiness in this world.

Thoughts can strike me here, swift and ruthless as divine punishment. Did I do that—scout the yachtie haunts, go out into Monaco to get information on my own—just to test him? To see if he could let go of his control?

Which would mean it was my fault. It was my fault that he was gone.

Black despair flutters up, taking benefit of every dark corner in my heart. I clench my hands in my lap until they're white. I look over at Mrs. Colding. What did she say? What did she tell me?

You will have what it takes when the time comes.

When the time comes.

"Where did they take him?" I say into the silence.

Mrs. Colding and Captain Redfearn jerk their heads up. "Pardon?"

I lift my chin, straightening my spine. "Where do they take"—I wave a hand—"Adrian's kind. When this happens."

Mrs. Colding draws in a long breath. "The clubhouse, in all likelihood."

I pinch the bridge of my nose. "Right. Their fucking yacht club. Of course." I clench my teeth. "And then what?"

Mrs. Colding sniffs, shrugs. "And then they try him for his crimes."

I swallow. "What could happen?"

Mrs. Colding glances at Captain Redfearn, and he takes over. "You saw the Shipwright. They take away his boat and let him fend for himself on land . . ."

"Or?"

The two veteran yachties share a look. "Or they leave him chained to a rock until the sun comes up."

The blood slows in my veins. "So where is this clubhouse?"

The captain looks at me.

A few minutes later, he unrolls a sheaf of old-fashioned sea charts on the dining table. I catch glimpses of names Captain Redfearn has penciled in himself, some of which I recognize. In Florida there is LAIR YACHTING, INC., and in the north TRANSMARINIA. In what must be Romania there is a place marked WHERE THEY CAME FROM?; in the North Sea off the coast of England, DEMETER SHIPWRECK. The farthest points of interest lie near Macau, China: a spot called THE PALACE OF THE FANG, and what looks to be an atoll named THE GRAVEYARD OF LAIRS. The swooping lines of sea routes connect all these locations, some of them expanded on with helpful little reminders and annotations. *(Summer only.) (Coven cruising grounds—avoid.) (Strange weather—Volok here?)* Captain Redfearn's notes on the . . . Lairverse?

But the captain doesn't linger on these. He pulls out another chart, this one a close-up of the Mediterranean. A callused finger points out an island in a bay along the eastern coast of Sardinia, also labeled in Captain Redfearn's crude chicken scratches: SANGUISUGA. Elaborating beneath and circled for emphasis: (*The Nosferyachtu Club*).

Good grief, how arrogant can you get? With a name like that, these undead fuckers weren't even bothering to hide themselves.

Almost as if they were daring to be found.

"It's been there a long time," Captain Redfearn says of the clubhouse. "You won't find it on any official map."

I gauge the scale on the sea chart. "It's only a day's passage from here."

Captain Redfearn nods.

"So the day after tomorrow, the sun might come up and burn Adrian to a crisp."

Another nod.

"Well." I look at both of them. "Seems we have until then to get him back."

They exchange a glance. Mrs. Colding's mouth twitches. Captain Redfearn straightens, eyeing me sidelong. "You're serious."

I blink, slowly, in confirmation. "I am."

The captain shakes his head, pacing in place. "You . . ." He snorts and shakes a finger at me. "Adrian chose well with you."

The ghost of a grin tugs at my mouth.

"How, then?" The captain gestures over the chart. "I can anchor in this bay up Sardinia's coast, but if we get any closer they'll see us coming. And we obviously can't approach by land." He shrugs. "By sea is the only way."

I hunch over the chart, chewing my lip. There's only one solution left.

"Then I take the submersible," I say, stepping back.

Captain Redfearn's jaw hangs. "You *what?*"

I shrug. "I take the submersible. I sneak onto land, create a diversion, and bring Adrian back."

Captain Redfearn looks at me as if I've gone crazy, throws up his hands. "Right. Of course." He snaps his fingers. "Easy peasy."

He looks at Mrs. Colding as if for help. But the chief stewardess is studying me with a sly look of admiration. "It could work."

"You mean—you think she can—"

"I do."

Captain Redfearn slides a hand down his face. "Okay, fine. Let's say you manage to get to the clubhouse without sinking yourself. Congratulations, there's gonna be a fleet of their boats waiting for you there. And if they're equipped with sonar detection, geo-fences, whatever—they'll see you coming miles off, and the game'll be over before it's even begun."

"What do I do, then?"

The captain shrugs. "Pray they're too arrogant to use them."

I purse my lips, nod. "I can do that."

Captain Redfearn sighs, rubbing the back of his neck, and glances at Mrs. Colding. She's already smiling at him.

I can't help it—I smile, too. "Let's go get my man back."

They laugh helplessly, like children, and once more I study the charts of the Lairverse. The Nosferyachtu Club looming large before me.

We sail through the night straight for Sardinia. We do not push for speed—we don't want to arrive too early and risk revealing our presence. I stand beside Captain Redfearn in the dark wheelhouse, the lights of the nav consoles casting a faint glow on our faces, and watch the bow of the *Lair* cut through the dark and seamless sea. Bringing me closer to Adrian.

At midnight Mrs. Colding appears at my elbow.

"Arie."

"Mmm?"

"*Arie.*"

I tear my eyes away from the restless dark.

"Get some sleep. You have a big day tomorrow."

I'm about to object when I see the grave look of concern on her face, and give in. "Okay."

Captain Redfearn gives me a reassuring smile as I leave. "See you bright and early, Miss Strand."

I wince a smile in return.

I'd been avoiding this—going to sleep, being alone. Because I know what's waiting for me. As I pad down the long hallways of the *Lair*, the safe numbness I'd felt in the company of others—the brisk distraction of taking care of business—begins to crack around a raw core of terrifying anguish. When I open one of the double doors to the master suite and see, on the bed, the iPad Adrian had used to buy our home, the grief takes me to my knees.

I fall asleep curled up in a ball on the bed, holding the iPad to my heart.

FIFTEEN

In the morning I scrub my face raw and tap my cheeks, bringing the blood into them. *Pull yourself together, goddamn it. Think of Adrian.*

When I answer the knock on the door it's Captain Redfearn, a strange twinkle in his eye. "Ready to be turned into a badass?" he asks by way of greeting.

The first step to badassery, apparently, is guns. Lots of guns. In a forward storage compartment, the captain glides a large metal cabinet aside like a hangar bay door to reveal a recessed wall mounted with an impressive array of weapons: long assault rifles and semi-automatics, pump-action shotguns, stubby pistols with rubber grips, even a bolt-action sniper rifle with a red-glassed scope.

I swallow. "Is all this . . . legal?"

Captain Redfearn snorts. "Fuck no. But when you're skippering for someone like Adrian . . ." He lifts a submachine gun off the wall and does that slick little cocking move you see in the movies, catches my look and shrugs. "I was a Navy captain before a superyacht captain." He sobers, eyeing me. "So I know a little something about fighting for those you love."

This brings a sudden lump to my throat. I meet the captain's eyes and nod, and he steps aside. "Take your pick, sweetheart."

I study the walls, the symmetric and strangely beautiful arrangements of hardware. *What the hell will help me for what I'm about to walk into?*

Then my eyes fall to the floor, and I point and grin. "What's *that?*"

Next, we move on to giving me a crash course on submersible piloting. The captain starts with general safety and diving theory, and then goes over the operational checklist again and again—ballast, life support, electronics and hydraulics—until my head is spinning. "You have to get this right," he admonishes as we sit in the sub in its storage locker. "We only have time to prep the submersible for one launch, so you don't get to practice first. This is it." So whenever he catches me in a mistake, I grit my teeth and tell him to go over it again.

After the dozenth mistake, however, it starts to get to me.

"Fuck!" I hiss, putting my face in my hands.

Captain Redfearn touches my shoulder. "Hey. I know you can do this."

"How?" I groan, feeling beyond pathetic.

"Because you remind me of someone."

I lift my face out of my hands. He's looking down at the instructions in his lap, eyes distant, looking like a gruff giant squeezed into a child's toy vehicle. Tenderness softens my words. "What was she like?"

He looks at me.

"Your daughter."

A gentle smile tugs his mouth. He takes a long moment before settling on the word. "*Tenacious.*" We both grin, and then he does something I would never have expected of him—he dwarfs my hand in his big rough one. "Nothing is beyond your abilities, Miss Strand. Of that I'm certain."

My eyes dart to him. I don't know what to say.

It's been a long time since I felt I had a dad.

"So," he grunts, changing the mood, and shakes out his instructions. "Emergency procedures?"

An hour before dusk the *Lair* drops anchor in a private bay. The engineer and deckhands have checked and triple-checked the submersible, and before long I'm standing in a black 3mm wetsuit on the tender boat with Mrs. Colding and Captain Redfearn, watching a crane swing the sub out of its locker and lower it into the sea.

Time to go.

I feel as if everything is happening too quickly. How are we already at this moment? Where did the time go? I am being swept along as in a dream, into bright uncertainty and terror. Air is suddenly in short supply, and I have to struggle to calm my breathing as I turn to Mrs. Colding and look into that comfortingly severe and composed face. I don't know what to say.

She doesn't need me to say anything. She hugs me tight, one hand cradling the back of my head. "Get him back," she whispers fiercely into my ear. "You hear me?

Make sure both of you come back. You do whatever you have to do."

I nod, tears springing to my eyes. "I will."

She pulls away, hands on my shoulders, and engages me in a stern, encouraging look. Perhaps it's only the wind whipping off the waves, but her eyes are bright and glistening.

"Ready?" says Captain Redfearn.

I incline my head sharply. I know that if I speak, I don't know what will come out.

I jump barefooted onto the swim platform of the submersible, undog the hatch at the top of the spherical glass cockpit and slither down inside into the pilot seat. Captain Redfearn follows me, his weight making the craft dip and bob on the waves, and peeks his head in through the open hatch.

"Remember," he says. "The Nosferyachtu Club shouldn't be far beyond that bend." He points a mile or so down the Sardinian coast to a craggy granite promontory jutting out into the sea. "Just follow the ridge beyond it, and it'll take you to Sanguisuga in the next bay. It should take you a full hour to get there. Be careful not to surface too close to the dock where the yachts will be. And try not to use your lights too much."

I nod as I pull my hair back into a tight ponytail and secure it with a spare hair tie on my wrist. "Got it."

"We'll be ready to disembark as soon as you get back. And I'll be on the walkie-talkie if you need anything."

I look up at him, touch his rough-knuckled hand gripping the rim of the hatch. "Thank you, Arnold."

He blinks at the use of his first name, opens his mouth and shuts it again. Then harrumphs deep in his throat. "Well. Good luck."

And he shuts the hatch.

I suck in a long, steadying breath and let it out in a low whistle as I take in the wealth of controls bristling at me. *You can do this, Aurora.* The world dips and bucks nauseously as Captain Redfearn shrugs off the harness on the submersible that's attached to the crane. Then he's leapt back onto the limo tender, and he and Mrs. Colding are staring at me like an old couple watching a child setting off on her own. On her way to a life that is beyond their protection. On her way to deeds she never knew she had in her.

I lift a hand, and they lift theirs in return.

Then I reach down to turn the knob that vents the ballast, and the submersible begins its descent into darkness.

SIXTEEN

I get used to it quicker than I thought I would.

Beneath, all is sublime quiet, a dire calmness through which drift the circling silhouettes of hammerhead sharks. I check the cockpit's navigation equipment, and before long its many knobs and buttons—the control of them—become comforting. After a few jerky tries my adjustment of the ballast tanks becomes more even, and the joystick reacts smoothly to my touch. Soon the shadow of the *Lair*'s hull fades away, after it the squiggly yellow blob of the setting sun, and before I know it I am drifting through inky darkness.

Night has fallen.

I flick on the submersible lights, twin beams igniting into the murk ahead, and keep to the shelf of submergent Sardinia falling away into the depths, low enough so that the lights won't be noticed above water. With the initial nervousness of piloting dropping away, though, my mind can wander. Which means I can start to think about what's ahead. About Adrian, and my chances of pulling this off. About how all my life I'd taught my romantic self to disguise my love, out of fear of losing it or realizing it had never been there in the first place. And how now I'm afraid that if I lose Adrian my heart will crack open.

Yup, better focus on piloting.

I check the diver's watch on my wrist. It's been forty-five minutes already. I'm wondering if it'll be obvious when I see that promontory when a wall of barnacle-encrusted rock hoves out of the gloom, and I have to jerk the joystick hard to starboard to navigate around it.

Jesus Christ.

I try to unclench my back and breathe, refocusing.

Shouldn't be far now.

I sit in silence, watching motes of detritus wicking past the submersible's glass sphere, its multi-jointed robotic arms looking like the mandibles of some mechanical tarantula. I have no idea whether I'm on the ridge or not; it's all monotonous seafloor crawling by. As the minutes stretch on, the doubt begins to creep in. Am I on the right track? How will I know when to surface off Sanguisuga? And how will I know that's where the clubhouse will be? Will I—

Oh.

For the lights of the submersible have flashed on something, picking it out of the murk. It's a bleached, almost luminous white, half-hidden in the silty seabed and waving meadows of seagrass. I feel the hairs on my arms stand up as comprehension dawns on me.

It's a skull. A skull is down here, with conger eels and colorful little fish darting in and out of its eye sockets and grinning jaw.

The blood drains from my brain. The breath rasps in my nose. My hand, slippery with sweat, pulls a knob to release a touch of compressed air into the ballast tanks, and I wait. The submersible rises up. The beams play across the climbing seabed. And I see it: an avalanche of skeletons, hundreds of them, tumbled in great heaps and ricks of bone along the underwater shelf, some of them recent, gray-skinned and staring with hair dreamily afloat, as if pondering what cruel fate had pitched them down here.

I think I've found the club.

My hands are clammy now, the blood thumping in my ears. *This is where they put the bodies.*

This is what happens to women here.

What could happen to me.

My tongue cleaves to the roof of my mouth. Sweat collects along my hairline.

Now the anger rushes in. Quick, efficient, merciless, knowing what's required. I flick the submersible lights off, plunging myself into darkness, though not alone—not free—from the afterimages of that graveyard all about me.

Time to ascend.

I close the vents on the tops of the ballast tanks and use compressed air to blow them clear of water, steadily enough so that I won't be shot like a popped cork to the surface. I look up at the moiling quicksilver of moonlight far above and close my eyes, shutting out the imaginings of bodies drained and tossed into the deep. *Get it together, Aurora.* The trick is to focus on my breath going in and out, long and slow like a competitive freediver, my eyes on that small glow above as if it were the light of heaven. As if it were Adrian. *I'm coming for you, baby. I'm coming.* And then the light is everywhere and the water above the canopy bubbles and froths and the Mediterranean night appears, framed in a dancing line of aqueous silver.

I've surfaced.

SEVENTEEN

I whirl to get my bearings, bracing myself to be paralyzed by a circle of blinding lights and shouting voices, tender boats full of sinister shapes. But all is dark and calm, the superyachts lined up blameless and unaware along a jetty jutting out into a bay a few hundred meters away, cables run out from them and hooked up to shore power. Seemingly deserted.

No one's spotted me.

Letting out a big breath, I turn to take in the clubhouse.

It looks deceivingly above suspicion. Shining warm and inviting in the night, nestled high up beyond the strip of beach on tidily pruned grounds backed by the silhouettes of trees: a many-windowed clubhouse looking like some cozy resort at Martha's Vineyard. At the head of a stone path climbing up to its huge red door, an innocent, white-painted sign lit by uplights: *The Nosferyachtu Club*.

Where else would a cabal of bloodsuckers meet?

The next step: Where to stash the submersible? I look about, and the answer is close: a huddle of coastal rocks that would hide it from view.

Bingo.

Now, only to get out and risk them seeing me.

I unscrew the hatch and inch it upward, one eye on the nearest yacht. No one about. All clear. I clip on a utility belt, sling a coil of double-braided nylon rope over my shoulder and lift myself out.

"Ohmygod, you're *so* bad!"

I freeze like a startled thief, heart hammering and half out of the hatch, as shrieks and giggles float over the water. Behind me, a tender boat packed to the gills with women in glittery nightclub dresses skims across the waves, coming from the looming hulk of blackness that is Sardinia. They're only fifty feet away.

I hold my breath. How can they not notice this ginormous submersible surfaced out of nowhere? They're going to see me. The mercenary-looking deckhands with their bulging biceps are going to see and they're going to reach for their crew radios and—

The tender boat skips by, its wake rocking the submersible in long, leisurely, nauseating undulations, and all is silent again.

Fuck me.

I shimmy out of the hatch and reach back down inside, slip a stainless-steel spike into a loop on the utility belt. Then I grab the long, rectangular weapons case that has been propped behind me in the cockpit this whole time.

Closing and dogging down the hatch, I lower myself into the water in one fluid motion. Even in my wetsuit the cold is shocking, and I take a moment to catch my breath.

Next, tying the rope to a bow cleat, and I'm striking out sleek and silent toward shore with the sub dragged behind me and the ribbed polyethylene weapons case floating alongside on the water. It's not long before we're in the sheltering cove of boulders. Struggling upright, I snick the slide spike anchor out of my belt—for that is what it is—and falling onto it with my whole weight I drive it into the soft sand in the shallows and tie it off with the other end of the rope. Sub secured.

Now the weapons case. I unsnap the latches, open it and lift out the six-shot revolver-type grenade launcher that's fitted into the black foam inside. First, I check it over for water damage. Then I unpin and swing the steel frame away from the cylinder in a break-off fashion, insert my fingers into the chambers and rotate the cylinder counter-clockwise to wind it and thunk the 40mm warheads home in the chambers. Then I close the frame and re-engage the axis pin to lock it.

Yeah, Captain Redfearn and I went over that, too.

Now I'm ready.

I have to take stock for a moment. *What has happened to my life? Who the hell am I?* Only months ago, I was on a farm mucking out horse stalls and birthing cows, and here I am now, girlfriend to a billionaire, the butt of a grenade launcher fitted against my shoulder and acting like a super spy.

No time to think about that shit now.

Clambering carefully up the sharp riprap of boulders tumbled along the shoreline, I peek over their tops toward Sanguisuga's jetty. The tender boat has glided alongside, and deckhands hold it in place with mooring lines as they offer a hand to the women hopping out. They giggle and pat at their hair, tug miniskirts in place, rings and bracelets and sparkly phone cases flashing in the dark. Some of them hop on one foot to get their stilettos on, and then they're being escorted up to the clubhouse, whispering excitedly to each other. Maybe it's because of this excitement that they do not notice the club burgee, vast and diabolic, rippling atop the front turret of the clubhouse.

Do they know what's waiting for them?

I know. For there's something else on the air, under the heady scent of Mediterranean herbs and the clean resinous smell of the pines. Something sweet and rotten.

It's accompanied by a low clicking, an almost furtive, insect-like cacophony rising above the blissful hush of waves.

It's not ten feet from me. A woman in a black sequined minidress, flung like a sack of garbage down into a crevice in the rocks. And she's *moving*. She's covered in hundreds of small crabs, a seething mass of jointed red crustacean shells. They scuttle over her bare arms and legs and cling in her hair snarled in black tendrils over her face.

Who knew the night of your life could be the night of your death?

I'm past nausea or revulsion now, or even a creepy-crawly shudder. All I feel is dull, permeating rage.

I tuck the grenade launcher against my shoulder and sight through its magnification scope.

A glimpse of the women inside, passing through finely appointed rooms containing vast gulfs of darkness. They're more subdued now, flicking glances to their left as they're hurried away by the deckhands. I scope over to the next window and see only a roaring fireplace in a large stone hearth. What are they looking at?

I need to get closer.

A quick scan tells me the yachts are still deserted, huge and gleaming in the moonlight like things better left sleeping. I dart forward, keeping low, to a manicured hedge not fifty feet from the house. I have a new angle now. Time for another look.

When I scope the windows again, I see Adrian.

My heart leaps into my throat. My breathing gets high and tight in my chest. He looks unharmed, still in his blood-spattered blazer and chinos, though his face is a stiff mask of defiant composure. He sits at the end of a long table lined with men with dark suits and wan faces. All of it has the feeling of a meeting of some secret society deliberating over deep mysteries. But I know what they're deliberating over.

One of the wan men rises. He has his back to me, and I wouldn't recognize him but for the red leather jacket he's wearing. He gestures toward Adrian and chairs slide back. All stand. Adrian disappears for a moment—my throat constricts—and then they're filing out of the clubhouse and down the stone path, Adrian in the middle with hands bound. I stiffen, blood racing. Are they going to the yachts? If they are, I can't make my move now. The yacht crews could come up on my rear. I'd be surrounded.

But if he gets on one of those boats, that's it. I'll lose him.

This is my only chance.

I hunker there, sweating under my wetsuit, frozen with indecision and the sense of grievous errors made, of everything falling part.

And then I'm saved: They take a turn, cutting along the shore. Some of them have electric lanterns, which they switch on now, globes of light floating through the dark. All is possessed with the solemnity of an ancient ceremony, like priests approaching a mountaintop oracle. Adrian is so close I feel like I can reach out and touch him. Every atom in my body strains toward him. My skin aches. I will him to look up and see me.

I'm here, Adrian. I came for you.

But he looks straight ahead, unseeing. He's led on and on, tragic and foredoomed, and I wonder, *Where are they going? Where are they taking him?*

The train of figures curves inland, straight toward a stained bluff mantled with spiny maquis scrub and the yellow flowers of helichrysum. And then they've gone *into* the cliff. Lanternlight flares up inside a jagged fissure in the cliff face, the entrance of an old sea cave. The lights bob, solitary and drifting, on and on into the awful darkness inside the world, like figures in a fable.

Then it's Adrian's turn to step inside. But he halts at the entrance, half-turning his head as if sensing something, and I lower the scope of the grenade launcher with trembling hands. I can't help it—I find myself rising from my crouch. Does he know I'm here? Does he know that I'm—

A pallid hand pushes Adrian on, and he vanishes inside the bluff, followed by the others.

Waves hush in the silence. A black wind presses down on me.

I grit my teeth and follow.

EIGHTEEN

Not far past the entrance to the cave darkness swallows me, and I rummage a pair of clunky night vision goggles out of a pocket on my utility belt. Captain Redfearn and I had decided against using thermal imagers—they operate off heat signatures, and so you need to be alive to be seen.

That wouldn't help me here.

I switch on the goggles and a shadow world propagates before my eyes, glowing with eerie green phosphor. Narrow walls curve away from me, shaped to hold the wind. Foul airs whistle in the silence. Somewhere, water drips and sings. Before me footprints lead away in the cold sand, rendered as silky white holes in a landscape of radioactive green, and I follow them cautiously. My bare toes sink into the grit. My body jerks with a shudder. It's cooler in here, and my face feels dewy. The damp air, I think. Or maybe that's just sweat from the terror beating like a bird in my throat.

At every turn, I expect to be confronted by the sight of some gangrel thing, ghoulishly green and eyes turned to glowing white orbs in my night vision goggles.

At any moment, I expect to feel a piercing pain at my neck.

But the passage curves on, seamlessly and endlessly, without incident. Here and there it widens, and I see the drip of water in pools of urned rock, pale newts with their little hearts hammering in tiny ribcages as they dart away across the gray loam. I'm beginning to feel as if I've been swallowed up in the earth's stone bowels when I freeze mid-step.

Voices. Voices echoing somewhere ahead.

They grow louder. They're coming from around a bend in the passage.

I take a deep breath and creep forward.

I smell the change before I see it. The sulfuric stench of saltpeter in my nostrils, urinous and pungent. Then the passage opens up and the light increases, turning everything into a blizzard of green snow.

I lift the goggles off my head to find out where I am.

It's a vast cavern hung with dripstone formations, stalactites twinkling with minerals. Those clotted arches seem to move, and I see that they're carpeted with dark and furry fruit. No, not fruit. Bats. They're bats, pugnosed and velvety black, lined up with leather elbows jostling as they murmur and squeak like mice in their sleep.

In the stone ceiling a hole, and through it moonlight slants down onto a small island in the center of a black and ancient lake. On the island, a monolithic slab of rock pointing towards the sky with a pair of manacles attached to it, its tall, broad face blackened by the ashes of old victims.

Adrian stands chained to the rock.

My heart leaps. The blood sings in my veins. The whole chamber behind Adrian blurs. His chin is held high, proud and undefeated. But there is a grim resignation in his eyes as he stares out across the lake. Crouching behind a limestone spire speckled with bat guano, I sight through the scope of the grenade launcher and follow his gaze.

There are many eyes glowing in the shadows on the far shore.

My skin contracts and breaks out in goose pimples. So, this is it. I must wait now in my hiding place and see how this plays out before I make my move.

A wind sighs through the cave, rank with the nitre reek of bat piss, and the trial begins.

A shadow stirs in the darkness. It glides forward with liquid grace, hovering at the edge of the moonlight haloing the island. When it speaks, it is in a thick Russian accent. "Poor Adrianchik," it whispers, the sibilant hiss echoing in that underkingdom like the call of a lover. "This very bad day for you, no?"

Adrian clenches his jaw.

"I was ready for big party in Monaco," the shadow continues. "Fucking women in ass before I decorate suite with their guts." A head shakes, a tongue *tsks* behind teeth. "But the great Adrian Voper decide to put end to fun with this"—the shadow makes a weary, languid motion with one elegantly taloned hand—"silliness." And a face as white and alien as the eggs of spiders glides out of the shadows into the faint moonlight. It has the harsh Slavic features of a man whose beauty borders on the cruel. "Yes," Radomir says, eyes glittering. "Very bad day for you, I think."

I find my throat has swelled shut.

"My father respected you, Adrianchik," Radomir continues, pacing along the shore. "Almost more than his first son." The Russian party boy's long nose thins. "Now, you are tragic figure. It breaks the heart."

Adrian stares at him with dully, baggy eyes.

"You do not speak?" Radomir places a hand to his chest and glances about with arch theatricality. "Is my English, no?" He smiles a thin, malicious smile. "You think after hundreds of years I learn English, or you Russian. But English"—he waves a finger—"is no good. Is impoverished language, unable to capture poetry of violence. Perhaps is why you do not speak? You let violence speak for you?" Radomir goes dangerously still. "But you need to give reason, Adrianchik. It is law."

Adrian's lips thin, and I feel my heart clench.

"Come, Voper. Speak and we may give clemency."

But Adrian does not speak and does not speak.

There's an angry whispering among the shadows, and Radomir turns his head to snarl out a ferocious noise that shouldn't come out of any man's lungs. Bats startle into the air, wheeling and chittering, and the shadows fall silent.

Adrian. So fucking stubborn.

At last, though, he lifts his head. His arms yanked taut above him, fists clenched in their manacles. "I couldn't bear it any longer."

Radomir cocks his head. "What is this?"

"*This*." Shackles rattle as Adrian pulls on them. "Being a criminal. A beast. Having to murder to survive."

Radomir holds himself very still. "Is not murder, Adrianchik. When you kill equals, *that* is murder. When you kill *them* . . ." He shrugs and dusts the air with his fingers, as if banishing a triviality.

Adrian's shackles clink as he strains against them. "I disagree."

Radomir favors him with a pale, thin smile. "It seem agreeable to you." He tilts his head back and forth. "For century or two." Then, hardening, "What change?"

This sobers Adrian. His trembling arms relax, wrists drooping in their manacles. "I did not feel . . . *anything*," he gropes, "for the longest time. And now that I've tasted that again . . . I cannot go on like this. I cannot *be* this."

My eyes water. My whole body grows heavy with a sweet, sinking feeling, overwhelming my senses.

But Radomir cuts through this. "So you decide to kill your maker." Adrian stiffens.

"Ay, yes. I know what you up to, Adrianchik. My father always know. He know you might come for him one day."

Adrian's teeth grit. He lifts his chin, his raised voice clearly meant for all to hear. "And yet your father—*our Commodore*—doesn't even have the courage to be here to give the sentence himself." Radomir's eyes narrow, but his composure does not break. He shrugs, the red leather of his jacket creaking. "Why would he?" And his sharp teeth gleam in a vicious smile. "Is obvious what should be done."

My heart floods with cold water.

The moment is here. I have to act. Intervention is required.

Get up, Aurora. Stand.

But my legs won't respond; they've turned to stone. Who do I think I am? Think of the hundreds of skeletons lying on the seafloor of the club's harbor. The horrendous strength and cunning it would take to do that—to get away with that—for centuries. Why do I think my fate will be any different?

Because it has to be. For Adrian.

Electricity races down my arms and legs. I'm attacked by pins and needles, a high and heady vertigo. And it is happening. I am standing on quivering legs and stepping away from my hiding spot toward the rimstone pool. My skin crawls, cold and exposed. The rustling of the bats above fills my ears. *Take a breath and step forward. You can do it. Now another.* In a moment I'll be in the light. In a moment they'll see me and there'll be no going back. Sweat moistens my brow, my hands gripping the grenade launcher, and my teeth clamp down to keep from chattering. I can do this. I will not falter. I will not freeze when they glide out of the shadows with mouths stretched wide in gentle mockery. I will not be a victim again.

This is it. Now or never.

I step into the light and open my mouth to shout it: *Let him go, or I'll bring all that rock down on your fucking heads—*

But I never get this out. I never start this sentence. Because—

"*But,*" continues Radomir, and my world contracts.

"Volok is willing to give you second chance," the Russian purrs. "He is generous man, and recognizes your . . . *standing* . . . amongst our kind. So, he gives you gift in hopes you be happy, and we can all be friends again."

And he moves aside to let someone step into the moonlight.

It happens as in a dream. I duck back into the shadows and behind a flowstone concretion, heart knocking against ribs, and lift the grenade launcher scope to my eye. A woman's face fills my vision. I've seen it once before, in a portrait in Adrian's suite. My breath sucks in. A high-pitched whine fills my ears. Something red and black explodes in my brain, and for a wild, irrational moment my finger tightens against the trigger of the grenade launcher.

Then the moment passes. The woman descends into the black mirror of the lake as if dipping into some unreal substance, her long green dress fanning on the water about her as she strides, all slinky sensuality and disastrous beauty, toward the island. Adrian looks like a man in the grip of a dream that defies all reason. He presses back against the rock he's chained to, eyes wide and deathly still, as the woman stops before him and touches a hand to his cheek.

"Hello, husband," coos Evangeline Voper with a small, tender smile, and it's as if all the air has been sucked out of the sky and bats are streaming out of the hole in the cavern ceiling in a great flapping of wings.

NINETEEN

I do not know where to go. I do not remember stumbling out of the cave, onto the beach. I am driven by an unspeakable need to not be seen, to not be found in this moment. It doesn't even have anything to do with the danger of being discovered by the Nosferyachtu Club members. It would be the shame to face *them*. Those two. Together.

Dimly, vaguely, it reverberates: the understanding that my life has changed.

I try it out to see if it sticks. If I can make sense of it. I think to myself, *It's changed, my life has been changed*, but I can't make sense of it at all.

All around me—battering my hair, pitter-pattering onto the beach—dried-out husks are raining down from the sky. Moths. The bats from the cave are at their feeding. They're bearing crazily down from the dark and swooping up moths in their tail membranes like vicious unmothers, crimped teeth flashing as they suck out their essence and drop them out of the sky.

The sight makes me avert my eyes, whimpering.

I find the sub as if by accident. I unstake the anchor and open the hatch and stow everything back in, very carefully, as if there is great importance in its arrangement. The grenade launcher huge and ridiculous—like a movie prop—in the passenger seat.

Pathetic.

What was I doing? Did I really think I was gonna swoop in and rescue him?

My cheeks burn with humiliation. How silly. How melodramatic and over-the-top to go through all this.

Silly little girl.

I push the sub out to sea and clamber inside and screw the hatch down tight, as if sealing myself away from the world. Away from everything.

Only then do I scream.

The passage back is a blur. The ascent, the tender boat motoring out to the sub bobbing on the dark sea. Captain Redfearn, white as a sheet, helping me aboard. "Are they here?" I find myself saying. "Is *she* here?"

But the captain does not need to say anything. Mrs. Colding waits for me on the swim deck, holding a towel and looking like someone has died. I chuck up my chin. "Where are they?" I whisper.

"Oh, Arie," she says. "Oh, baby."

"Where are they?"

In the dining lounge. They look up when I come in, still in my wetsuit, water dripping from me and pooling about my bare feet. They're seated across the dining table from each other, hunched over and hands close to touching, as if I've interrupted an intimate moment. When Adrian sees me, he pulls his hands away and lurches to his feet. "Aurora," he says, as if he doesn't know what else to say.

I do not answer.

Adrian swallows and glances at—*her*. "I'll see you in the morning."

She nods, rises to her feet and looks at me. I glare right back. She tries a tentative smile and vanishes down the hall in the direction of the guest cabins.

Adrian stands there a long moment, unable to quite meet my eyes. "Are you okay?"

I don't even know what to say to that. I stare out a window, and he swallows in regret. "You must be cold and exhausted. Do you want to change out of—"

"No."

He flinches and nods, glances at Mrs. Colding and Captain Redfearn waiting behind me on the aft deck. "Let's talk in the master suite."

When we step inside, he shuts the door and goes to sit on the bed. He waits for me to join him, but I remain standing, arms crossed. He slowly rises again. "I heard you came for me—"

"Is she staying?" I blurt out.

He takes in a long breath, holds it and lets it out. "Can I explain?"

"By all means."

He nods, presses his palms together as if in prayer, eyes shut, and then begins. "She didn't die."

"I can see that."

"I didn't know."

"Then why didn't she come forward before now?"

He sighs. "Because Volok enslaved her."

It comes out small and unbidden, as if I've been gut-punched: "Oh."

Adrian begins to pace, head down and shaking. "You've seen how my kind treat women. There's no place for them as one of their own. So they put them to work, carrying out tasks they deem too tedious to carry out themselves. But now she's back, and she . . ." He stops, covering his eyes with a hand.

I lift my chin, feeling a sudden stab of pain behind my eyes. "I see."

"I thought she'd died, Aurora." He comes to grip my arms, and they tighten across my chest. "I . . . I just need time to think, okay?"

"To think," I say.

"Yes."

"About what? Getting back together?"

His hands drop. Hurt fills his eyes. "What? *No.* It's just—"

"What? It's just what, Adrian?"

He sighs. "She's my wife, Aurora. I can't just turn her away."

I take in a long, shivering breath, feeling a hot flare of shame despite myself, and nod. "What about going after Volok?" I look at him. "That hasn't changed, right?"

He shakes his head, laying a cool hand on my cheek. "Of course not. But the Nosferyachtu Club made it clear:

I take Evangeline back and accept being a vampire, or they destroy me. So I have to at least play along with it for a little while. Give us some time to come up with a new plan. Okay?"

I shift my weight, biting my lip. The word is pried from me in a whisper. "Okay."

He draws me into his arms and I stand there with my cheek pressed to his chest, my fingers curled uncertainly into his shirt, my heart beating a staccato roar as I try to push back the tears that want to come.

TWENTY

The three of us have breakfast the next morning. I feel as if I've been knocked into a light, breezy space. All looks as normal and yet like a spiteful mockery of itself. The sparkling sea, the aft bridge deck banquette with its terry cloth cushions propped against the chrome rails, the dining table with its rolls of silverware and wooden chargers and vase of white lilies. Mrs. Colding dipping about us, mouth pinched in a hard line, as she darts looks at me. Adrian, my Adrian, looking as if he hasn't gone through any ordeal, as if nothing has happened, he was not kidnapped and almost sacrificed to the sun and I did not try to rescue him with a grenade launcher. The only thing different—the one blinding exception throwing my world out of true—being the woman with her quick and easy laughter and her smiles, sly and knowing, that have a way of holding something back.

She is not how I'd thought she'd be. I had expected a woman serious and cold, unapproachable behind a veil of austere beauty. But her beauty is very much approachable—magnetic, even. Her seductive cat eyes, her sultry swagger. And, of course, those perfectly molded waves of blonde hair. She has the sophisticated charm I've wanted all my life, her style simple and elegant: an eye-catching black one-piece with a plunging neckline, sunglasses covering most of her face. Her voice deep, confident, insouciant. She sits with her long legs crossed, her head often thrown back in delighted laughter. A drollness there, yes, a flash of thought that is not shared with the outside world, but it is becoming. Alluring.

She fusses with Adrian. She tugs on the sleeve of his billowy white Ralph Lauren shirt. "You dress differently now."

"Yes." He flicks a look at me. "A lot has changed."

She takes in the meal, the flowers, his shirt. "I see that." Then she follows his gaze. She makes a show now of solicitousness. She invites me into her world, her attention like a benediction as she snicks her sunglasses away and rolls her eyes. "What you must think of me, showing up like this after so many years."

I swallow the lump in my throat. "I understand."

"It was the hardest thing I've ever endured, to be kept from him," she says, tossing Adrian a darling look. "And when they released me to see him at his trial . . . well, it was a miracle."

"Uh-huh." The word dries up in my throat.

She turns to me, reaches a hand across the table. "I know this must be hard for you. Thank you so much for allowing me to be here."

I force a bright smile. "Of course."

Adrian glances between us, looking as if he's not sure where to put his eyes. Mrs. Colding, hovering to the side, clasps her hands very tightly together.

"It means so much to me to be able to see Adrian again," continues that woman. And she flashes a dazzling smile at him.

I struggle to keep my face a mask of politeness. "I'm sure." And I reach out across the table and hold Adrian's hand, snapping Evangeline's eyes there. "We're happy you're here," I simper. And then, smiling wider, "We're very happy."

A moment as our eyes meet, before she twitches her head, bird-like, in a smile, and gestures vaguely. Mrs. Colding dips forward and Evangeline holds up her cocktail glass. "I'll take another."

"Right away, miss."

"Mrs."

Mrs. Colding turns back, her face carefully composed. "Pardon?"

Evangeline looks at me as she says it. "You'll address me as Mrs. Voper." And by the slight but intentional shifting of her hands I notice, for the first time, the gold wedding band on her finger.

Mrs. Colding's lips part. She startles a look at me, but I do not return it. I'm too busy listening to the blood roaring in my ears.

"I adore the lilies," Evangeline is saying lightly. "Even if they are a little lackluster for a yacht."

I'm trembling when I march inside into the main lounge, hands on hips. Mrs. Colding follows me and touches my shoulder. She is white with fury.

"I know, dear. I know."

"What is happening? How can he be *letting* this happen?"

She doesn't know what to say to that. She holds me and rubs my back, shushing me. "I don't know. He'll figure it out soon. He will."

They chat long into the evening, catching up on each other's lives. She had spent the years as a cleaner at the Nosferyachtu Club, mopping up after the parade of models lured to that seashore hideaway. Her hands and knees stained red from scrubbing at the floors, tossing the bodies into the harbor. A century of quavering terror and servitude. "I never stopped thinking of you," she assures Adrian, her voice clogged with tears. "I tried to escape many times. But they always caught me." Having no phone or a way to contact the outside world, she tried getting word to Adrian through the visiting club members—but few of them knew Adrian, lone wolf that he was. The ones who did were too terrified to cross Volok. And so she was left to suffer, watching Adrian from afar, gleaning hints of him over the years, and like him tried to forget herself in frenzies of feeding.

It's all so perfectly, tragically romantic it makes me want to puke.

Adrian, listening, quivers with rage.

"But what of you?" she asks, changing the subject with a brave show of self-deprecation. "Tell me everything."

She listens intently to his account. His isolation, the unyielding rigidity of his life. When he haltingly gets out the part about him gorging on blondes over the years, she touches his hand. "Oh, Adrian," she whispers.

Adrian flies a panicked look at me.

"But Aurora saved me," he adds quickly, and fills her in about us. About all I've done for him. Evangeline gives me a long, considering look with a winglined eye from behind the curtain of her blonde hair, and changes the subject again.

There comes a time where I have to leave them lying there side by side on loungers on the sun deck, overlooking the nighttime sea, and retreat to the bar to make myself a gin and tonic. The ice rattles sharply in the glass. My hand shakes as I pour. Somehow the feeling all around me, which I cannot escape. I am interrupting. I am an interloper. I no longer belong here.

"Miss Strand?" The mousy new stewardess, the one I traumatized, stares at my shaking hands. "Can I get that for you?"

I glance at the gin sloshed onto the bartop and flush with embarrassment. The stewardess— Corinne?—gently mops up with a napkin, and I'm overcome with a glistening of sympathy. Not so long ago

I was in her shoes. Not so long ago I was subject to the whims of an owner I did not understand.

How so much can change, and not really change at all.

When I glance at the benighted stretch of sea behind us, another yacht rides the darkness, port and starboard sidelights aglow. Is it following us?

Later that night, I lie in bed stiff and unmoving as Adrian holds me. "It's okay, you have nothing to worry about," he whispers in my ear. "It's only for a little while, and then she'll leave."

"Promise?"

"I promise." He brushes a lock of hair back from my face. "I trusted you, remember? Now it's your turn to trust me."

It's enough for me to soften in his arms and fall asleep, dreaming of the impossible loveliness of the woman in the guest suite down the hall. Of Evangeline Voper and the lies we tell ourselves.

TWENTY-ONE

My sleep is shallow that night, plagued with dreams at turns distressing and shockingly lustful. I dream I am running after Adrian down an endless hallway in the *Lair*. I run and run, but when I catch him he turns to me with a stranger's wide, unsettling smile. *Hello, Evangeline,* he says. *My love, my love.* And when I see myself in the mirrored glass of the hallway, it's not me. It is, indeed, Evangeline. I have been Evangeline all along.

The crickets wake me. The crickets of Oregon, rising to a buzzing, razzing roar, deafening and indefatigable, and I am in bed with Josh again. *See?* he says. *You'll always be mine,* and reaches for my bare flesh.

I wake to the hush of the sea in my ears. I'm panting, my heaving chest glossy with sweat. Stranded on a dry patch. Unwelcome lucidity. I watch Adrian's face, concentrating on the curve of his lashes on his cheek to block out the sick, shameful itching between my legs, and a sudden twisting of my gut wrenches me out of bed.

I need some fucking chocolate.

I slip out the door and pad down dimly lit hallways toward the galley, the pants of my silver silk pajamas swishing against each other. The yacht is quite cool and still at night, the moon outside the windows high and drifting in the cloud-scudded sky. We've dropped anchor at sea, but where I don't know.

I haven't known where I am for some time, it seems.

Glancing out the windows on the bridge deck, I check to see if that yacht is still following us. A light bobs amongst the swells, but it's too distant to make out what it belongs to. *You're being paranoid, Arie,* I remind myself, and pad on.

The galley. Its many surfaces gleam silver in the dark, like some space age cockpit. The ovens, the range hoods, the dumbwaiter. I've cracked the fridge and am squinting in its sudden glow when I hear it: a scrabbling sound, a weak thumping as of fists against metal cabinets, and over it—faint and petrifying—a wet suckling.

A delicate sweat breaks out along the insides of my arms. My breathing gets high and fast in my chest. The skin at the back of my neck suddenly feels cold and exposed. I don't want to turn, don't want to know. But it's worse—far worse—not to.

Taking in a long, trembling breath, I force myself to twist around and see what's waiting for me on the far side of the long kitchen island.

Evangeline, in a man's t-shirt and fluttery silk charmeuse shorts, kneels over Corinne lying on the galley floor, the stewardess' eyes wide and staring as the last twitches jerk her body.

So. Someone else wanted a midnight snack, too.

I make a sound. I must make a sound, for Evangeline lifts her head to look at me, eyes flat and black as an animal's in the sterile glow of the fridge, and wipes the blood off her chin with a wrist. "Oh, hello," she says in a cheery and comradely way. "Excuse me, just finishing up."

Just finishing up. Corinne—mousy, empathetic Corinne—with two dainty holes in her neck.

Daintily murdered.

Oh, hello.

The fridge door snaps shut—its light winking out and wiping away that image—and I barely have time to lunge aside before I'm dry-heaving, one hand on the kitchen island, the other on my knee. I spit and wipe my mouth with the back of my hand. "What the fuck?" I hoarse, voice rising. "What the fuck is wrong with you?"

Evangeline pauses, flicks a wrist. "What?"

"You can't just—snack on the crew whenever you fucking *feel* like it!"

Evangeline shrugs an elegant shoulder, rising now into the pale moonlight streaming through the galley's round windows. "Hey, no one told me, okay?"

"No one *told* you—"

She rolls her eyes, lifting her hands. "Every boat's different, all right? I didn't know Adrian was so attached to—"

"What? *People?*"

She smirks, hands on hips, her cat-like eyes surveying me. "You really are something when you're flushed."

This clicks my jaw shut. I take a sharp breath in through my nose, a sudden, bewildering rush of embarrassment overtaking me, and try to steady my breathing. I'll be damned if I'll let myself look like this in front of her.

Evangeline's mouth curls in amusement before she changes tack. "I suppose that frigid Mrs. Colding woman is off-limits, then?"

I give her a look, and she shrugs. "One can dream." She strides past me and opens the fridge, peers inside with a huff of boredom. The sound of someone settling for second best.

Nowhere else for me to look but at Corinne (*the corpse*) on the floor. The two trails of blood curving down her neck and pooling in a cherry red puddle beside her. But it's all right—what I feel awaken in me is just a cool and spacious curiosity.

"What's it like?" I ask when I can speak again.

Evangeline is thumbing blood from the corner of her mouth. She arches a brow as she glances at me, plucks out a saucer of chocolate mousse. "I don't know. What does power taste like?"

Power. Perhaps that is what I envy in this woman. That feeling of invulnerability that gives you the charm and carefree wit I once thought beauty gave you. That staggering, self-glorying sort of beauty that unquestionably attracted—and still attracts?—Adrian.

But I could have that. I could have all of that if I became like her. Like *them*.

If that's what I wanted.

No. I push this away with a queasy upwelling of disgust. *What am I thinking?*

But Evangeline knows. There's no middle ground for us, it seems. Nothing between chilly formalities and overwhelming intimacy. She is staring at me with slitted eyes as she sucks a dollop of chocolate mousse off a spoon. She gestures with it between me and Corinne's body. "This can stay between us girls, yeah?"

My jaw unclicks. You gotta be *kidding* me.

But still. A high and giddy clamminess, some ancient and canny instinct, keeps me silent. Evangeline's mouth cracks in a sly smile. "That's the great thing about women. We know how to keep our secrets, don't we?"

And before I can protest, she's stepped close—much closer than courtesy allows—and lifted elegant fingers to feel a lock of my dark hair.

I hold my breath.

"You're very pretty," she says at last, silky and confiding, and I feel an absurd pleasure, an inexpressible wave of flattery wash through me. All this before she adds, "I'm glad you were there to keep Adrian happy while I was gone."

And she herself is gone, spooning chocolate mousse deliciously into her mouth as she struts off with her ass cheeks shimmying in her fluttery shorts, leaving me in that galley-turned-morgue where the very air vibrates with trespasses.

I wake Mrs. Colding and Captain Redfearn to deal with the body.

They're not pleased about it—either to be woken or to hear the cause for it. When Mrs. Colding stands over the corpse and stares down at it, her nose thins, and a delicate bloom of color appears in her cheeks. But she does not say anything. It is Captain Redfearn, hands on hips, who speaks.

"So this is who we're dealing with."

The fellowship here, the feeling of us as a team, still makes me dizzy with relief. "Do we tell Adrian?"

Mrs. Colding gives me a look. "You think that would go over well, do you?"

Point taken.

The chief stewardess draws herself up. "Don't worry about it. The captain and I will take care of it. We have it from here."

They've had a lot of practice in this area, after all.

Captain Redfearn fixes me with his gaze. "Be careful. This one's dangerous."

I do not sleep for hours. I lie in bed beside Adrian, rocked by waves of uncontrollable fury. That sneaky bitch, already at it with the head games. Putting me in an impossible position where my humiliation and hard small anger is both complex and unmentionable. Because that is precisely what she's counting on. I cannot mention it, as Mrs. Colding warned. If I did, I'd risk pushing Adrian away, making myself look jealous and petty.

Which means I have to live with it. Live with what she did, and her drawing me into the dirty business of dealing with the body and keeping it secret from Adrian, the wrongness of it all clinging to me like a grave odor.

This is my enemy.

TWENTY-TWO

It begins all over again the next day. The long talks, the laughter, the inviting leans of the ear. And all the while, I am thinking of Corinne. I am thinking of the sounds Evangeline made—feral, voluptuous, engorged with blood—and this polite and laughing nonsense now. The two-facedness, the preening hypocrisy. Gloating.

There's only so much I can take, so much I'm willing to take. A red mist of fury and disgust has come over me by the time I grab Adrian's hand. "We're overdue for our couple's massage, aren't we?" I stand, feeling Evangeline's eyes on me, but refuse to look at her. "The masseuses are ready."

Adrian raises a brow, but does not say anything, does not protest.

Because, of course, there are no massage therapists on the *Lair*.

When I close the door to the sauna behind us, I turn to peer at Adrian through the silky vapors clouding the space. Condensation beads on his skin, slipping down the broad planes of his pecs, his sharply ridged torso. I suddenly feel like a teenager again—jittery, trembling, hoping he finds the luscious bikini I'd chosen enticing. "I thought we were overdue for some alone time."

He smirks, knowing what's expected here, and leans in. I lean in, too, letting my breasts brush against his chest. I tip up my face so his moist lips can slide across mine.

Much sooner than I'd like, they pull away, drawing a sigh out of me. "I've missed that."

He smiles but does not say anything, and silence gathers in that dense and sweltering air. I have a sudden fear that if I speak, fill that silence with pretty, inane words, it'll only feel hollow and forced. Nothing like their conversations. Their connection.

So I focus on the real reason I brought him here.

"So," I say, glancing out the sauna's steamed-up door and biting my lip. "Now that we *are* alone, we can talk about Volok."

His face slackens, grows long. My stomach knots. He hoists himself up onto a sweating cedar board in a bulging of triceps, head lowered, and I have to force away a flutter of doubt as I plop myself beside him.

"Obviously, our plan will have to change now they know you're after him. I was thinking—"

"Can we talk about this later?"

I blink. His tone is light, carefully remote. It crushes me.

"Oh. Yeah. Sure."

I push the fear away, firmly, that he's avoiding talking about Volok. That it means anything.

He nods, his mind already moving on. "The snow room?" His expression is strange when he suggests it. There's a hopeful determination about it, or even a sly challenge. These are what my thoughts have come to.

"Sounds nice," I say.

It's even more freezing than I'd feared. As soon as I tiptoe inside that freshly snowed winter cave, my feet go numb. I have to cover up that failure of a bikini and huddle in a fluffy white robe, teeth chattering and cheeks blue as I shiver on a stone ledge beside him. He turns a mild smile on me, impervious in his swimming trunks. "You sure you're okay?"

"Puh-puh-perfect," I chatter, huffing fog and feeling every square inch of my skin harden up into goose bumps.

Adrian's rubbing my back when the inner door to the snow room swings wide and the breath leaves my lungs.

Because a glistening and butt naked Evangeline has just romped in.

My cheeks burn; a riotous buzzing fills my head. But I cannot look away. There's simply no looking away from a body like that. It's *unbelievable*. I would *kill* for that body. As in premeditated murder. I suck back drool and stare, smoldering with awestruck envy. It's as if, after all these years, Evangeline Voper is still in the flush of youth, poised deliciously in that first dew of maidenhood. Her skin is as soft and white as the snowflakes about us, her breasts like pearls, her legs never-ending, her lips as red as heart's blood. It's unfair, and maddening.

It's Evangeline.

"Oh," she says with false coyness, and turns slowly before us, showing off her lush figure as if emerging from a boudoir. "I didn't know you were in here."

Her eyes never leave Adrian's face.

And he is staring. Sitting there beside me, staring. It must be a vision to him—what he had lost so long ago, returned to him.

When I look up Evangeline is watching me shiver in my robe, pointedly composed and unaffected by the cold. She places a hand on one sultry hip. "You all right, darling?"

My jaw clamps. The blood roars to life in my veins. I stand, letting my robe slip off my clenched and rigid body, tendons cording in my neck, and meet her eyes. "Fine," I snap, and snatch Adrian's hand. "We were just leaving."

I am brimming over with rage by the time I halt my march. We're halfway down the hallway to the master suite, and Adrian watches me as I pace back and forth. "I know what you're going to say," he begins.

"Do you?" I scoff.

"She's European, okay? That's how she was raised."

"How convenient," I spit.

But he stops me, rubbing my arms. "I'm sorry. I'm sorry you had to put up with that."

Damn fucking right.

I wait, pouting, wanting more. But he doesn't give it. He kisses my brow. "I'm gonna shower. You should warm up, too."

I watch him go, hugging myself, gooseflesh crawling my arms. I'm still like that when Evangeline drifts up beside me in a robe and crosses her arms, following my gaze. "Having a moment?"

I glare at her. "I know what you're up to."

The points of her eyebrows draw together. "Oh?"

"It won't work."

Her lips upturn as she feigns ignorance. "Whatever do you mean?"

I roll my eyes. "Please." I gesture at her. "I know what that—*display* was."

"Oh, honey," she tuts, touching my shoulder, and gives me a once-over. "I know it's hard. It's natural to worry. For women it's natural. The pressure we're under. Age comes for us all, and soon enough things begin to sag and wrinkle." Her eyes rove over my flesh, and my arms tighten instinctively over my chest. "For women, for mortal women, life goes in only one direction. For men, they can start all over. They have choices. The fresh young lover, the new wife. Can we really blame them for straying? It's how they hold on to their youth, after all."

I can feel it happening, her dizzying concern battering at me, drawing up the contrast. The inevitable conclusion.

I wonder what she's going to say next, what heady new sympathy will emerge.

"I feel for you," she goes on in her maliciously kind way. "I really do. I'm thankful I don't have to worry about such things anymore." She lets out a tinkling little laugh before dropping her voice to a respectful, commiserating hush again. "But you needn't worry about me. I may have this body forever, but I can tell yours makes Adrian happy. And who knows, maybe he won't notice you aging. I'm sure you two have the kind of lasting love that'll make him overlook all those little disappointments. Isn't that right?"

Our eyes meet, and we both smile.

"Thank you, Evangeline," I simper.

"Not at all," she purrs.

And she struts away, leaving me to stand there with hands fisted at my sides, as if I wasn't even worth recognizing as competition.

We'll see about that.

TWENTY-THREE

I get ready before I lose my nerve. I'm trembling with rage, and not a small amount of wonder. What a fucking talent, to be able to compliment and insult in the same breath. To reassure someone and destroy them all at the same time.

But I have my tricks, too.

I shower and oil my skin to a high sheen, curl my hair in dark waves around my face. I go bold with my makeup, harshly accentuating my eyes and lips. Last, I choose a tiny black thong bikini I've never had the guts to wear. I study myself in the mirror, chin lifted. I look like a goddamn porn star.

"You can do this," I tell my reflection.

I find them in the beach club. They're lying on loungers in the shade of the opened garage door, their voices low with laughter. When I strut past into the sunshine on the swim deck, flaunting all my carefully manicured flesh, Adrian goes mute mid-sentence.

He's still a man, after all.

I grab a bottle of lotion as I loll on a sunbed, ass cheeks to the sky. "You gonna rub me down, baby?" I call lightly, then make a show of remembering. "Oh, that's right. You can't."

Evangeline's eyes narrow to slits of purest black. Adrian cocks his head, torn between amusement and offense.

So I take the plunge. I pass the bottle of lotion to a deckhand stationed nearby with hands clasped behind his back. "I guess someone else will have to do it, then."

Adrian's lips thin. The deckhand flicks an uncertain look at him.

"That's all right," I say, snapping the deckhand's eyes back to me. "Don't worry about him. You don't want me to burn, do you?"

This last as I stare at Adrian. He gives me a dark look, as if to say, *Are you really doing this?*

I am. I am determined to meet his eyes, despite the blush that's flooded my cheeks. Despite feeling absolutely ridiculous.

"Mr. Voper?" ventures the deckhand, uneasy.

Adrian is still staring at me when he says it, his voice soft with scornful indifference. "Go ahead."

The deckhand's throat bobs as he grasps that this is actually happening. He has a bad case of the shakes; it takes him a few tries to open the bottle, squirt out a dollop of lotion. He must be

younger than me. No more than a boy, really. He looks terrified but faintly aroused as I roll over and stretch like a yawning cat, baring my tight stomach. Waiting.

I am trembling all over now. I peek an eye at Adrian. His hands white-knuckle the armrests of his lounger, his eyes a glittery black as he watches the deckhand lather up my torso. Evangeline smirks, but it fades when she sees Adrian's expression. I shut my eyes and writhe luxuriously, biting my lip. "Mmm," I moan as the deckhand's rough hands grip my hips and swirl up my ribcage, fingertips brushing the undersides of my breasts, setting off in me a quivering of nerves.

It's too much for Adrian. He shoots to his feet, the muscles in his face jumping, held back by the wall of sunlight dividing the beach club and swim deck. Evangeline tugs his arm, shaking her head. *Come on.*

It takes considerable effort for him to master himself, but he does. He begins to turn away, and I cannot allow that. So I do what have to.

I pull at the string of my bikini top and it all but pops off, letting my breasts bounce free. Adrian freezes. The deckhand gapes, darting a terrified look at him. But I grab one of the deckhand's wrists—our eyes lock—and slowly move it up my body until his hand is cupping my breast. The deckhand swallows, his eyes golden with astonishment. He knows this is a mistake, that he's in a whole heap of trouble now. But he is too overwhelmed by the heady urges of youth, his unbelievable good fortune at this hot chick offering up the pleasures of her body, to resist. And so he moves up his other hand. Soon my tits are gleaming with nipples perked and hard, and I feel a tingling between my legs, humiliation and disgust burning beneath my skin. A sickening vertigo takes me. *What am I doing? How can I let another man touch me like this? What have I become?*

But I push this away. This is what's required now.

This is what I tell myself as Adrian and I lock eyes. His chest is heaving, his hands fisted at his sides. Evangeline looks between us, face set in ugly rage, and melts into the gloom of the beach club. Defeated.

Almost there.

I arch my back and moan, writhing under the deckhand's hands, and—

"Aurora!" The word lashes like a whip, yanking the deckhand away. Adrian jabs a finger at his feet. "Come *here.*"

I prop myself up on my elbows and arch a brow. "What if I don't want to?"

Adrian's eyes blaze. He swivels his head to the deckhand, teeth clenched. "Bring her to me. *Now.*"

I can feel the deckhand trembling when he grabs me. He yanks me up and marches me like a mulish child over to Adrian. As soon as I fall within the shaded overhang of the beach club, hands grip my arms with bruising strength.

"I ought to—"

"What?" I say, glaring up into Adrian's face. We are inches apart. "What ought you to?"

Adrian stares into my eyes a long moment, quivering with rage. Then crushes his lips to mine.

The suddenness of it overwhelms my senses, obliterating all thought. When he pulls back there is a taste of blood in my mouth.

He grabs my hand. "You need to be taught a lesson."

It's a blur to the master suite. I cannot breathe. The blood is singing in my ears. I am almost out of my skin with a rare and terrible elation. Before we're even to the bed Adrian is tearing at me, pushing me down. We have never been so rough with each other, so without caution. He pins me on the floor, growling curses into my ear. He fills his hands with my breasts so recently known by another man's hands, taking a nipple in his mouth, setting all my nerve endings afire. He is reclaiming me. He is making me his again, and the savageness of it makes me achingly wet. I should be afraid, I know. Given my past, I should be afraid of this roughness, this voracity close to violence. But I'm not. I'm exultant. I watch him, open-mouthed, my hands tangled in his hair. He bites at me, nipping my flesh like a dog, and it does not even occur to me how close we are to him giving in and turning me. That is not what I'm thinking about. I'm not thinking at all. My body is one big burning need. I tug at his belt with trembling hands, fumbling the buckle with a hiss of impatience. He grins and helps me, and in a moment he's inside me, shocking me—as he always does—with his fullness. "*Fuck*," I groan, deep in my throat, as I shut my eyes and arch my head back. Then I'm wrapping my legs around his strong back so I can pull him in deeper, my arms around his neck. I croon to him, urging him on. I say filthy things I never would have said before. It has the desired effect. It drives him into a frenzy of passion, surging lean and powerful as a swimmer between my legs, making me glow with pleasure. This is what I wanted. This is what I've wanted for what feels like so long now. At one point I straddle him, and over his shoulder I see—through the door we've left open in our haste—a shadow watching us. Evangeline. Evangeline is watching us from the hallway.

I'm not shocked, like I think I'd be. On the contrary, my blood cools. I dig my nails into Adrian's back, my eyes boring at her with contemptuous triumph over the bulk of his traps. *Mine.* Even this satisfaction, though, cannot compete with the faint sense of despair and corruption in the room. In our lovemaking. *This is how*, I think. *This is how we destroy love.*

I hold Evangeline's eyes until Adrian shudders and cries out beneath me, and only then does Evangeline melt away down the hall.

Our passion has left Adrian and I spent. We fall asleep at once and when Adrian wakes he has me again. He is full of a new consideration and tenderness and he kisses me goodnight with what seems to me a strange and newfound sympathy.

What has become of us, Adrian? What has that woman done to us?

When I wake later that night, I am alone in bed. Adrian is gone.

I jolt upright, gripped by cruel premonition. I spring out of bed, my heart hammering in my chest. It's mere moments before I'm out in the hall before the door to Evangeline's suite, lifted hand trembling. What will I see?

Nothing, it turns out. The suite is empty, unnervingly spare. No clothes lying about, no sign at all of anyone residing there. Even the bed is neatly made.

What?

That's when I hear the piano playing drifting through the dark yacht.

I stiffen. The music is beautiful, austere, feminine—not Adrian's.

Of course.

A slow processional ascending to the library. I'm in no hurry now. I can take my time. Whatever I'm about to see will be there waiting for me. I feel myself a solemn and doom-laden voyeur, dutifully fulfilling what is expected of me.

I come to the library door and creak it wide.

She is playing. Seated at the blackly gleaming baby grand, Evangeline is playing. And Adrian is watching her. He stands behind the piano, leaning toward that music—closer and closer—as if under a spell. She does not watch her hands dancing on the hard white keys. She stares into his eyes, and the look they share is somehow more naked—more intimate—than if they were in bed together. It's as if what I'm seeing is a hallucination, a snapshot of the past—her playing in the glow of the footlights, and him falling in love with her for the first time as adoring roses are flung out of the dark onto the stage. The room, unaccountably, has the air of a bridal suite.

I do not know what to do. I cannot go into that room and put a stop to this. I cannot go back to bed knowing what is going on above me. What's unfolding here is too all-encompassing, too obscene for that. I grope away through the dark hallways of the *Lair* and out onto the deck, thinking, *It is happening. It has happened.* The side rail now, its stainless-steel cool to the touch, and I'm sucking in a huge lungful of air and clamping one hand to my mouth to stop the sobs from coming out and undoing me.

A pawn. I've been a pawn. I've been driven to covetousness, to petty acts of jealousy. Who would want that, when they could have a bewitching creature who can play such gorgeous music? Who, if given the choice, would choose me? Isn't Evangeline what every man wants? They encourage women to be sluts, to be the fun girl, but at the end of the day they'll leave her for the kind of woman whose sultriness is sophisticated, who makes their desire feel decent and respectable. This is the lot of women.

And the sobs come now, slipping out between my fingers, bending me over. The tears squeezing out of my eyes and dropping onto the deck.

No. That's not true. He got upset because he loves me. Hold to that.

I straighten and wipe at my cheeks, shake my hair out of my eyes.

Remind yourself: *I can't think this way.* Remind yourself: *I have to trust him, remember? I can't let my past relationship affect this one. This is Adrian. He loves me.*

I have to trust him. Trust him. Trust.

When I at last return to the master suite, I pull my pillow over my head to block out that private performance of Evangeline Voper. I do not remember Adrian coming back to bed.

When I wake in the gray dimness of morning, my world has changed.

TWENTY-FOUR

The *Lair* is filled with the scent of roses.

TWENTY-FIVE

It's true. My white lilies on the nightstand are gone, replaced by a vase of lusciously red roses exuding sweetness like a heady, overwhelming perfume. This continues out in the hall, on the decks, a sickening hallucination. Roses everywhere. I tear through the *Lair*, feeling as if it has turned transparent, my life transparent, thrust under a sudden clarifying lens. How can everything still be standing?

And there's a ringing in my head, endless and piercing. As if someone were striking, over and over, a high piano note.

I find Adrian in the main salon going over the books with a frigid-looking Mrs. Colding, surrounded by boxes of furniture. I don't recognize the change at first; I have to sidestep a circus of deckhands lumbering past with a hideously expensive crocodile skin sofa. Then it wallops me in the stomach like a brick.

A suit. He's changed back into a suit.

Back into his old, protective, controlling self, back when he was with *her*.

I have to take a moment to recover from this. And then the anger returns. "What is this?" I snap, gesturing at the lurid red flowers festooning the place.

Adrian's face grows taut for a moment, his eyes flicking toward the aft deck. Then he turns a page in the ledger he's holding. "She said she wanted to do some redecorating. I didn't know she was ordering those."

I glance through the tinted glass doors onto the aft deck. Evangeline is out there in a big floppy sun hat that dips elegantly over one eye, overseeing deckhands switching out deck cushions like an imperious art director. Awareness comes into her shoulders and she glances back at me, the faintest of smirks on her lips.

My ears burn.

"You do know this is her trying to edge me out, right?" I round on Adrian. "You do know that."

Adrian doesn't look up from the ledger. "Don't be ridiculous." He points to something on the page. "And when are these flown in?"

But Mrs. Colding doesn't notice. She's locked eyes with me, and I sense a kindred feeling of outrage. Adrian notices her distraction and relents. "It's just for a little while. Once she's gone, it'll change back."

I feel a disastrous pressure of tears. "And how long *is* she staying, Adrian?"

Adrian's jaw muscles dance. "I thought we'd agreed you'd try to trust me."

I snort. "So she's not going anywhere, then."

He shuts his eyes and draws in a long, calming breath. "This has been hard on her, too. We need to make this easy for her—"

I bark out a harsh, humorless laugh. "Hard on *her?*" I shake my head, a wild recklessness taking me as I gesture at the boxes of furniture everywhere. His suit. "This isn't you. She's changing you back to what you were before."

His eyes shut again, teeth gritting. "That's not true—"

"I thought you didn't want to be this anymore—"

"*Careful,*" Adrian says in a warning voice.

"And now what? You're just going to let Volok win?"

The ledger snaps shut, cutting me off. Adrian's nostrils flare as he jabs a finger toward the *Lair*'s immense windows. "You see that?"

I turn my head to look. We've entered the Strait of Bonifacio, headed toward Corsica. For almost as far as the eye can see delicate blue waves glisten with painful brightness in the sun. And there, following us at a discreet distance, a medium-sized superyacht, unremarkable yet vaguely chilling in the lack of life on its decks. I feel my arms prickle.

"It's been following us since Sanguisuga," Adrian explains. "Since the Nosferyachtu Club."

What? My jaw drops. I turn to Mrs. Colding, gauging her expression.

It's true.

She hands me a pair of binoculars and I glass the boat. The national flag of Germany at the stern, the courtesy flag of Italy at a starboard antenna. And then I find it, fluttering brazenly from the bow staff in a rippling of inverted white triangles—the familiar burgee of the Nosferyachtu Club.

My chest grows cold.

We don't care that you know, that flag says. *We want you to know we're following you.*

"I knew it," I mutter under my breath.

"They're watching us, Aurora," Adrian continues in cold summation. "It would draw too much attention for Evangeline to leave so soon. What do you expect me to do?" And he turns back to his ledger, clearly done with the conversation.

Mrs. Colding and I eye each other sidelong, both of us thinking the same thing.

We'll just have to give this Nosferyachtu boat the slip, then.

TWENTY-SIX

The boat stays on our ass all the way to Corsica.

My body thrums with little flashes of disquieting excitement. I can't concentrate—my thoughts on my conversation with Adrian keep unraveling at the sight of the yacht gleaming in the sun behind us. I don't know what to feel. But it comes through, all the same: the relief. *That's why Evangeline is still here. That makes sense. That's all it is. He's keeping up appearances so we can get out of this.*

Almost strong enough—almost—to quell any lingering doubts in my mind.

Now I can allow myself to wonder, *Where are we going?*

Rounding a bend along Corsica's coast, we come upon an island with a bay that looks like some lost paradise: crystal clear waters, a beach like a scarf of white silk, lush green mountains protecting the spot from all cardinal points. There are already a scattering of yachts at anchor in the bay, tenders ferrying guests out to the stone houses and restaurants tucked back amongst the hills.

When we drop anchor, the Nosferyachtu boat does the same across the bay from us.

My heart pinches in my chest, and I share a look with Mrs. Colding standing in the wheelhouse beside Captain Redfearn. We have to come up with something.

But it's too late. Adrian is stepping out onto the shaded gangway with me, telling me to be ready at sunset. We're going ashore. Evangeline thinks we need to get off the boat, get some air. And I think, *The first fucking thing we've agreed on.*

I can't say I have a good feeling about it.

Lights are winking on along the curve of beach by the time Captain Redfearn taxis us ashore. As I hop onto a wooden jetty, I can hear laughter and gabbling voices, the sounds of people having a good time.

But we don't head that way, like I expect.

Adrian leads us across the beach toward the thick forests of pine and cork oak blanketing the island. He's changed into a sharp blue suit that makes me think of a naval officer, and Evangeline walks beside him in a long flowing white dress that gives her the look of a bride. I find myself trailing after them like a lost dog, bare feet floundering in the deep sand. I throw a bewildered look behind me at Redfearn in the limo tender, and he shrugs. He's as lost as I am.

When we cross into the forest tree line, full darkness descends like a shroud.

All I can see is the full moon glowing as white as a lemon ice above the clawing branches, feel the duff of matted pine needles under my feet. I stumble over roots and through tangles of maquis scrub, feeling like an idiot, while Adrian and Evangeline, with their unnaturally sharp eyes, walk on in dreamy perfection ahead of me.

An undefined humiliation is setting in. My cheeks burn red in the dark as we amble on, my head filling up with a hot clot of angry thoughts. Why this island? Why this fucking forest? Do they just want to stretch their legs?

But that can't be true. There's always more with Evangeline.

And they're speaking now. Endlessly, incessantly, they whisper to each other. They point out the timeless charm of this place. The glimpses of stone ruins that we pass, Roman cisterns and towers and crumbling walls overgrown with moss and ivy, the vestiges of some lost estate. It is all like a dream. A dream of a time long past. And it is, for them. They speak of it. They are still speaking.

"Remember that time we . . .?"

"Remember when . . .?"

"Isn't that where we had . . .?"

And on it goes, Evangeline leading him down a road of nostalgia paved with glittering highlights. The good old days. Back when they were together. Wasn't it marvelous?

Here and there they turn to me, including me almost out of a feeling of guilty obligation, or pity. As if I would want to be included in this.

"Do you like this? Would you like this? Isn't it perfection?"

A creeping foreboding clutches me. I can't wait any longer. I have to know.

"Have you been here before, then?" I ask lightly.

Evangeline glances back at me, a small smile on her lips. "Oh, didn't we mention? This is where we got married." And she points to an old stone gazebo on a windswept promontory, desolate and lonely, on the high cliffs of Corsica overlooking the sea. "Right there, in fact."

The already dim world seems to darken briefly. The blood booms in my ears.

Adrian won't look at me.

I can see it. The two of them, in that blue suit and white dress, striding from that gazebo into a waiting crowd of adoring friends, hunching their heads and laughing as rice is thrown into the air in a joyous white confetti. I sway, feeling suddenly unsteady on my feet. I know Adrian sees it, too. His eyes have gone distant as he relives the memory of that day. It brings a sudden surge of hot vomit into my throat.

"Well?" Evangeline probes, snapping me out of it. She is glowing with malicious anticipation. "A beautiful spot to be wed, isn't it?"

"Yeah," I manage, ignoring the pulse ticking at my eyelid, my voice heavy with sarcasm. "Lovely."

Evangeline drinks this in, as if my insult is a reward, an outcome to be celebrated. Then she turns to Adrian. "Shall we go on?"

Adrian stiffens, obviously thrown by this suggestion. "Go on?"

Evangeline's smile dazzles in the darkness of the pine forest. "I have a surprise for you." Adrian glances ahead, back to me. "Going on might be painful for Aurora—"

"I don't mind," I blurt.

Evangeline gives me a pitying look. "You may be right," she says, pouting her lower lip. "Maybe you should sit this one out, Arie—"

"No." I take a step forward, tilt my head back and meet her eyes. "I'll come along."

"Perfect," Evangeline trills through a carnivorous, triumphant smile. Adrian looks between us, face tight with dread.

A strange transfer of power has occurred. After this conversation Adrian sinks into a subdued trance, as passive and tractable as a child, and Evangeline takes the lead with motherly tenderness. Anxiety prickles through me. I follow like a ghost, in numb disbelief. As we leave the cliffs and that accursed gazebo behind, I wonder what Evangeline has in store, what horrible surprise will be revealed.

It is not at all what I thought it would be.

After a while the forest thins, and the path leads us out onto another strip of sand. Not a beach, though. A narrow sandbar or tombolo leading out into the sea, and which ends in a rock escarpment jutting upwards at a dizzying angle. And perched atop that unlikely roost is a house, tall and lonely, haunted-looking against the night sky.

My skin contracts in foreboding.

I know. I instantly know what I am looking at.

"Welcome," Evangeline says as she turns to me, gesturing with a smile, "to Voper Manor." My heart thuds against my ribs. I look at Adrian. I can't decipher the expression on his face as he gazes up at that edifice. All I know is I never want to see it again.

Evangeline, all teeth, takes Adrian's hand in hers and leads him forward.

I feel as if I have fallen into a paralyzing dream as I follow. My feet are lead weights as they shuffle me across that sand causeway flanked by hissing surf. The house looms, taller and taller, circled by crying seagulls and backed by the glowing enormity of the moon. A beautiful nightmare. After the fashion of Corsica, it is built in a single block so it looks like an extension of the crag it stands upon, with dark green roof tiles and small openings in its façade to limit the entry of the wind and sun, almost like a castle. Unlit, unlived-in for over a century, the ivy creeping up its walls giving it the appearance of a decaying corpse. Their house. The house they lived in, as newlyweds, in a life that does not belong to me in any way.

Theirs.

Then we are hiking up the escarpment to the very doorstep of that place, and Evangeline grabs the knocker on the front door—a band of iron clenched in the teeth of a snarling face—and swings wide.

A ponderous creaking. For a moment Adrian hesitates on the threshold, glances back at me. As if he knows that if he crosses it, something will be found within that he can never escape from.

But Evangeline does not allow second-guessing. Resecuring her grip on his hand, she drags him in. And like a helpless dreamer, he follows.

So I, too, in turn follow.

Given the cavernous space within, I expect our footsteps to echo. They don't. The house gulps them down. It is muffled and dark with vegetation in here. Ivy and vines snake through the windows and cover the stonework in a thick tangle of knotted root. Dust furs tapestries and faded coats-of-arms. Rats scurry in the corners. Bats wheel and flit through the moonlight stabbing through the parts of the ceiling that have fallen in. I glimpse upper reaches hung with candelabra shrouded in spiderwebs and wonder if Adrian lived up there as a boy. It occurs to me, suddenly, that this house is where he took his first steps, spoke his first word, had his first crush, and a painful tenderness squeezes my lungs.

Then Evangeline drifts forward, gazing about at the grand ruin. "What times we had here," she says softly, wistfully. "So brief, but so happy."

The words stab me in the heart. I think of Adrian carrying her up those stairs to a bridal suite. I think of their laughter, the sounds they must have made later.

She stops before something in the middle of the room, large and dappled in shafts of moonlight. The vines twisting up its legs and over its lid obscure its shape, but my throat tightens all the same.

When Evangeline folds back the case with a creak, the ivory keys of the piano grin in the dark like the smile of a lover.

My heart pangs once, hard, in my chest.

"Maybe they don't have to be lost," she says, depressing one key so she can listen to its lonely note fill the house. It's slightly out of tune, but still lovely. Haunting. She smiles to herself. "This place could be saved. We could renovate it."

The idea—the pure, sickening grotesqueness of it—makes me gape.

Evangeline looks about, that smile still twisting her lips. "We could redo the roof, put shutters over the windows. Maybe, eventually, we'd move in from the *Lair*—"

"Okay, that's enough," I snap, unable to take it any longer. The disgust and outrage that's been building inside me comes bubbling out and I place my fingers to my temples, feeling as if my head is about to explode. "This—this is beyond fucked up." I whirl on Adrian. "You're seriously okay with this? Taking you here. Parading you through your old home together. Suggesting the two you—you—play fucking house again! And doing it right in front of me. How can you go along with this bullshit?"

I'm panting by the time I'm finished, waiting for his reaction. Evangeline waits, too, a glint of worry behind her aloof composure.

At last, Adrian glances toward the door. "Maybe we should—"

It's not enough. It's not nearly enough. I roll my eyes and round on Evangeline, hands on hips. "Why are we here? Really."

Evangeline's cheeks dimple in a repressed smirk, as if my outburst was exactly what she'd been hoping for. Then she covers the keyboard once more. "Follow me."

She saunters off across the tangle of roots covering the flagstones, hips swaying hypnotically. Adrian hesitates a moment, shooting me a profoundly uncomfortable look, then follows her, and I trail after with my head held high, burning with embarrassment and the unavoidable feeling that I've made a mistake. At the rear of the house is a small rotting door overgrown with ivy and studded with iron. When Evangeline grates it open in a squeal of rust, salt spray and the cries of gulls slap me in the face. It feels wild back here. Unpredictable. I expect a straight drop into the sea, or perhaps a forbidding garden of spiny cacti clinging to the cliff. Instead, there are steps carved into the rock, winding down the sheer cliff face.

"Mind your step," Evangeline calls over her shoulder as she vanishes down them.

I exchange a look with Adrian, asking him with my eyes. *What's down there?*

But he does not tell me. His face like stone, he follows his wife down the steps carved into the living rock of Voper Manor, and I follow with my heart in my throat.

It does not take long before the steps end in a doorway that's nothing but a shape of darkness leading inside the house's foundation. Above it is a slab of stone, a lintel of sorts. An architrave chiseled with a single word: VOPER.

A sudden panic grips me, and I reach for Adrian. "Wait—"

But it's too late. He's already disappeared inside.

My pulse thuds in my ears. Water booms against stone. Seabirds hover in place on the wind, letting out cries of aggrieved warning.

I suck in a deep breath and step inside the awful dark below Voper Manor.

The sting of salt in my nostrils gives way to the smell of earth, moist rock. I reach out and slide my hands along the walls in here, feeling my way forward like a blind woman in the blackness. I'm in some narrow corridor moaning with the wind. There's no knowing how safe it is, how deep it goes. My footsteps echo loudly in my ears, and I think of Evangeline down here, her pale face rushing out of the gloom, befanged and demoniacal, and a sudden, overwhelming fear of treachery and ambush leaps up inside me. "Adrian?" I try once, sharply.

But there's light ahead. It flickers and dances, a bright and hungry orange.

Evangeline is waiting calmly at the end of the corridor, a lit torch in hand, like some icon out of an old story. Adrian stands before her, a haunted knight errant, bent by the burden of his quest.

I stop, wary, my hands balled at my sides. "What are we doing down here?" I grit out.

Evangeline, unblinking, serene, turns away from me.

"I was going to tell you on our wedding night," she says, addressing Adrian, the words dull with controlled emotion. "During our last stroll on the deck of that ship, in fact. I thought it would be the perfect wedding gift, to tell you we were going to have a child."

No. The thought rolls through me, vicious and instinctual. *Stop talking. This can't be.*

"But then Volok bit me, and the baby . . ." Her face falls. "It died when I did." A wind moans down the corridor, whistling eerily, blowing her hair into her eyes and making the torch flame gutter and cast wild shadows. Her chin quivers. "I was so ashamed . . ."

It is very hard to tell in this fitful dark who moves first, but suddenly Adrian is holding Evangeline's hand, squeezing it in comfort.

The sight twists at my soul.

"I felt I should show you," Evangeline says, this gesture seeming to give her the strength to go on. "I felt I should show you where I buried our daughter." And when she sweeps her torch so its light plays over the moist wall, I realize that the stone my hands had been gliding across in the dark has turned into crypts, dozens of them, stacked in neat rows up to the corridor ceiling in a vast honeycomb of death.

We are standing in the tomb of the Voper family.

And there on the plaque of a crypt too small for an adult, letters glinting in white marble, recently inscribed: ANGELINE VOPER.

Goose bumps pebble my skin. A terrifying spaciousness opens within me.

At last, Evangeline turns into Adrian's arms, clutching at the lapels of his suit as she summons up tears worthy of a tragic play.

I cannot move. I cannot breathe. It's as if the air has been punched out of my chest. The horrific sound of Evangeline weeping soaks into me like poison, corroding my insides. For I know. I know that this unassailable move has laid a claim on him I cannot touch, shutting me out entirely. No one can match the fusing intimacy of that kind of grief. If she was relying on one thing to draw him back into the sentimental familiarity of their relationship, this would be it. Her winning card.

How can I fight that?

Adrian clumsily caresses Evangeline's hair, his face a frightening blank as he holds the torch for her, and suddenly I cannot watch this scene anymore. I stumble away, leaving those two cocooned like fiendish saints in their halo of deranged torchlight, and claw my way back down that corridor filled with the moaning wind and the bones of Adrian's forebears, my gorge rising in my throat. I need out. I need air. I am stumbling, scrabbling, whimpering, and then I'm exploding into the fresh air on the threshold of that tomb where everything is crashing waves and the crying of gulls and I can feel it working upon me, a lightening of things, a strange and terrifying exhilaration: I have been robbed. I have been freed of my life.

TWENTY-SEVEN

The return to the *Lair* is unbearable.

I trail after them across the pale sweep of sandbar and back to the island in a daze. My whole body is achy from stress, my eyes fastened with helpless misery on what's before me: Evangeline, walking with her head on Adrian's shoulder and an arm around his waist, her footsteps as heavy as a sleepwalker's with the drowsiness of spent grief. Adrian rests an uneasy, comforting hand on her, glancing back at me in the moonlight as if to ask, *Are you okay?*

What can I do but nod back?

My head fills with an ugly rage, fierce and vengeful, uncompromising. Far behind me, seagulls cry in sorrow or disappointment, pulling my eyes back to the baleful silhouette of Voper Manor towering before the incandescent face of the moon, and I have a brief, violent desire to see that ruin crumble and crash into the sea.

The gall of it, for her to orchestrate this. And with me here.

Has it worked then, as I feared? What is Adrian thinking now? What is going on in that gorgeous head of his?

What will happen next here?

I'm bracing myself for further performances, further exploitations—why doubt at this point that the worst could come to pass?—but Evangeline doesn't press for more. She stops at the old stone gazebo where they were married and wipes sleepily at her eyes. "I think I'll take a walk. Clear my head."

Adrian hesitates, as if reluctantly surfacing out of a fond melancholia. "Okay."

She offers a wan smile and wanders off toward the gazebo, and I have to marvel at her show of noble mourning. It's impeccable.

Adrian stares after her a moment, before becoming aware of me watching him. He slips his hands into his pockets. "I'm sorry you had to—"

"It's okay," I mutter. "I understand."

He nods, unable to look at me.

"Are *you* okay?" I ask. "Do you want to talk about—"

"That's all right," he says, a little too quickly. "I just need time." "Okay."

We walk in awkward silence back to the beach, stand in the sand and watch the *Lair*'s limousine tender drift at the jetty, Captain Redfearn's mane of silver hair flashing in the moonlight as he waits for our return. We don't know how to look at each other. Finally, Adrian snaps out of it. "Do you want to—"

"That's okay," I blurt. "I think I'll take a walk, too."

He nods, unable to stop the relief from coming into his face. "Okay." He turns to the lights along the beach, that relief blurring into something else. "I should hunt," he says, soft, as if to himself. "I haven't fed in a while." He gives me an almost shy glance. "See you soon." And he trudges barefoot across the sand toward the brightness of the village and what waits for him there.

Leaving me alone.

All the pent-up rage and anguish I'd been keeping in floods out of me in a rush. I suck in a sob, fluttering a hand to my mouth, and shut my eyes. I am trembling. I am full of wild and childish hate for my predicament, for the pitiless uncertainty gnawing at me. What am I to do now? I feel myself on a razor's edge, surrounded by pitfalls. If I push too hard I could lose him. The thought of having to say goodbye—of having to give up on him—makes my knees want to give out. I'm not ready for that. God help me, I still love him. So how much space do I give him without letting her sink her claws in deeper?

Her. Her. Her.

I scan the bay to see if I can annihilate that Nosferyachtu boat with the force of my glare, send it up into a conflagration that would light up the night with righteous destruction, and find it's nowhere to be found. The waters are dark where it had been moored. It's gone.

Or moved.

My heart drops. Ferocious suspicion blazes up in me. I whirl about, casting my eyes at that dark mass of woods humped up against the sky.

The woods where that gazebo would be. And where Evangeline went.

My jaw clenches down hard.

I stumble through the woods in a mad daze, maquis scrub and pine boughs tearing at me, cutting my arms and legs. I have to know. It only takes me minutes to get to the gazebo. I rock to a stop at the edge of that giddy promontory, the wind flying my hair into my eyes, and look down. Below me, gentle surf breaks against the cliff face. And beyond, dark stretches of sea, unlit and lifeless.

No yacht to be seen. No Evangeline.

Of course.

I'm about to turn away, chiding myself for being an idiot, when I see it.

A flash of light on the sea. A signal.

There's a boat out there.

And when I see the signal again, it illuminates something fluttering from the flagstaff at the bow, an ensign flag with a pair of white and rat-like fangs on a black field: the burgee of the Nosferyachtu Club.

Goose bumps break out all over my arms.

And when I look down at the shoreline to see what the boat is signaling to, I see unfurlings of white gown glowing in the moonlight, blonde hair blowing in the wind. An apparition.

Evangeline.

It has to be Evangeline. Walking out to the tumble of boulders on the shore. Waiting for a tender that's now pushing out from the Nosferyachtu boat, a dark figure at the bow.

My heart thumps in my chest. Why would she do this when she had been finally freed from Volok? Why would she be sneaking around?

I have to get closer. I have to witness this.

There's a narrow path, steep and dangerous, descending from the cliffs to the rugged shoreline. The path Evangeline must have used.

Hunching low, I scramble down, bare feet quiet as a thief.

The tender is halfway to shore now. Evangeline positions herself on a rock ledge, waiting, like a figure in a painting.

Adrenaline surges through me. I'm so jittery I nearly lose my footing and careen into the sea. Hugging the cliff face, I hop down onto the shore and creep close, lift my head so I can see over a boulder.

The boat has reached Evangeline.

The figure disembarks and approaches her, almost gliding. From here, I can't make out its face. Only its outline. Narrow, masculine, shoulders hunched up all but to the ears. Is that her lover? Is that Radomir?

Is that . . . *the Commodore?*

The hairs on the back of my neck stand on end.

Evangeline bows, and then the two bend to speak to each other, hushed conspirators.

"You were right, Master." Evangeline's voice, a tone in it I haven't heard before. "It's working. I just need a little more time."

My heart leaps into my throat. I'm so blinded by the lurching righteousness of the betrayed that I forget for a moment: I should take a photo.

Sweat pushes out of me. My hands are shaking so much I nearly drop my phone.

Then I lift it and snap. Once. Twice. Three times.

Got ya, bitch.

Hot, exultant rage consumes me, but I force it down. I have to concentrate.

The other figure responds, but I can't make out the words over the sound of the waves. I have to get closer.

Heart hammering in my throat, I round the boulder—and slip, sending rocks clattering.

The two figures on the shore jerk their heads my way, and for a moment their eyes flash like silver discs at me, eerie and reflective as a predator's in the moonlight.

My whole body goes cold.

Wild, animal terror takes over. Before I know what's happening, I've turned and am hurtling back up the cliff with my heart in my throat, the sweat pushing out of me. Is she behind me? Is she coming? Then I'm at the gazebo, in the woods, branches tearing at me, and it's suddenly very clear how fucking stupid it was to have followed a vampire into a wood, at night, alone. *What was I thinking?* The woods seem to go on forever, a blur of bark and pine needles, and my panic doubles. *Did I get turned around? Am I going the right way? Did I lose the path?* I hear the snap of a twig and whirl about, breath hitching, straining my eyes to see in the gloomy crowding trees. Was that a glimmer of white gown flitting from trunk to trunk? Was that the glint of teeth as sharp and long as a wolf's? Was that the glowing eyes of the undead?

By the time I've burst out of the trees onto the beach I'm sobbing, bleeding, covered in scratches, and I all but fly into Captain Redfearn's arms. The grizzled skipper holds me, stunned. "What is it, sweetheart?"

But I can't tell him. Not now. Not yet.

Because Adrian won't believe what I've seen. I need more before I present him with this.

I need evidence.

How do I get it, though?

My arms harden up with chickenflesh, and I look past Captain Redfearn to the *Lair* floating in the dark.

Time for a more thorough investigation.

I hesitate before the door to her suite and look about. I don't know when she'll be back. But I have to know. I must have some time.

I have to know.

I creak the door wide, fumble along the wall for the light and flick it on.

The change in the room since last I saw it is startling—she's turned it into a Mr. and Mrs. Voper memorial. Vases of bright red roses scream from every corner. Fresh sheet music is laid out in neat stacks on an ottoman, written in a clean, elegant hand that looks scratched out by a quill. And last but not least, a gold locket lies open in a place of prominence on the night table—portraits of Adrian and Evangeline as newlyweds.

It's so sickeningly manipulative it makes me want to scream, but I can't say I'm surprised.

I wonder if I'll get my surprise in the walk-in wardrobe, and creak the door open.

I have to stand there for a moment taking it in. The contrast couldn't be more pronounced: While the main room is the model of style and cleanliness, the closet is a catastrophe. Clothes are heaped everywhere, flung carelessly askew on hangers or spewing out of luggage in a bright vomit of color all over the floor. It's over-the-top, obscene, like the messy dark side of a mind that has been shoved away from the light, and I get the sense that I've stumbled upon the true Evangeline Voper.

And then there are the bodies—what Evangeline must have been feeding on while she's been aboard the *Lair*—sprawled in a bright splash of blood amongst the clothes.

I suddenly feel sick, my skin sticky with sweat. I know, with sudden certainty, that I shouldn't be seeing this. It's not safe for me to be here.

I have to get away.

But straight ahead of me is a small black safe. It's sitting on its own on a shelf of dark wood like some kind of idol. And it's ajar, as if its owner had to leave in a hurry.

A dark thrill of dread and celebration shoots through me.

Every nerve in my body is jangling, telling me to turn, to flee, to not see what's in that steel box. But I can't. A deeper need urges me on. I step forward, breath held, over twisted limbs I will not look at. My bare feet crackle in sticky pools of dried blood. The stench of rotting meat assails my nostrils.

My hand lifts. I grip the door of the open safe and draw it wider . . .

Revealing the black screen of a phone lying inside the safe.

My heart leaps into my throat. She claimed she didn't have a phone, didn't she? Why would she lie about that?

Then I think of her visitor on the shore, and it all makes sense.

I'm beginning to tremble now. It's all there. All the secrets, all the answers, contained in that phone. My hand throbs, pulsing with too much blood, as I reach inside the cool space of the safe, feeling as if I were plunging my hand into the dark maw of a garbage disposal, waiting for its blades to whir to life and—

RRRR.

The phone vibrates and lights up with a text, making me jump. I have to put a hand to the middle of my chest to stop from screaming. *Jesus Christ.* But I can't look away. There's a name there, on the illuminated screen. I can almost read it. It says—

"Are you snooping, Arie?"

I almost slip in the dried blood as I whirl, my heart galloping under my hand. Evangeline stands silhouetted in the doorway of the walk-in wardrobe like some nightmare out of my subconscious, her waves of blonde hair haloed by the light from the passageway outside.

My flesh frights up, but I steady myself by gripping my phone in my shorts. "Just curious why you'd be meeting someone from that boat from the Nosferyachtu Club."

There follows a period of grim silence.

"What did you say?" she purrs.

I shrug a shoulder in affected nonchalance. "I mean, what would Adrian think if he saw this?" And I show her one of the photos on my phone.

She stares for a long, long moment. I glow with triumph, waiting for that smug expression to melt off her face—but that never happens. If anything, it flickers with amusement before she flies a hand to her chest, eyes wide with theatrical distress. "Oh my God, you're right. That's *so* incriminating. You should *totally* show Adrian."

My insides sink. I turn my phone about.

It's the same photo. The same shoreline with its breakwater of boulderstones gleaming in the moonlight.

And there, on that rock ledge where Evangeline and her shadowy companion should be—nothing.

What?

I flick through the other photos, but they're all the same. No Evangeline. No phantom lover.

Nothing.

"Oh honey, you seem to be confused," Evangeline clucks. "You sure that's what you saw?" The world seems to droop around me, flooded with hot embarrassment. Beads of sweat spring out on my brow as I take a step back. "No. I *saw* you—"

"I'm sure you *wanted* to see me. That would have made it easier, wouldn't it?" Evangeline shakes her head, oozing disappointment. "It hurts me to know there's this rift between us. After being so vulnerable with you today, I thought we'd come to a new place in our relationship. What did I do to make you think this of me?"

It's an effort to breathe. To think. Maybe that figure I saw wasn't her. But it must've been. That dress. That hair. And that boat putting in to shore with its passenger. Had I hallucinated all of it?

My legs feel weak, I feel as if the floor has opened up beneath me, that I've come upon a horrid drop. A sensation very much like insanity.

"No," I manage at last, shaking my head. "You met up with them. You're—you're in fucking cahoots with them somehow. And you've been communicating with this—" I snatch the phone out of the safe, press the side button to show the text on the home screen.

But it's not Radomir's name there. Not Volok's.

It's Adrian's.

And the text reads: *See you soon.*

All the warmth leaves my body.

"Sometimes we need to communicate," Evangeline explains, a tiny, wicked smile flitting about her lips. "We didn't want to hurt your feelings." She leans forward in maddening benevolence and squeezes my shoulder, mouth pouting sympathetically. This is how she keeps me from finding my footing. "I'm sure you understand."

And it's not over yet. A shape is materializing behind her, stepping out of the shadows: Adrian with a body slung over his shoulder. The body of a man. This man has no color in his face. He is not breathing.

"Hey," Adrian says, looking between us. "Everything okay?"

"Everything's perfect," Evangeline says, calmly plucking her phone out of my fingers. "I was just telling Arie that we were about to feed."

Adrian gives me a guilty look. "I'm sorry."

And when they stand there looking at me, I realize they're waiting for me to leave, like two parents informing a child it's time for the adults to be alone.

"Of course," I find myself saying, a flush creeping into my cheeks. "I'll . . . leave you to it." I slip past them and out the door with my head hunched into my shoulders, feeling Adrian's apologetic gaze on the back of my neck. And when I stop in the passageway and turn back, the body has been laid out on the floor and Adrian and Evangeline are kneeling, each with a wrist held to their mouths, the still-warm blood oozing down their chins and filling that room with the smell of fresh-poured iron. And as I watch, Evangeline lifts her eyes to Adrian and smiles over her wrist with its bubbling puncture wounds, and Adrian smiles back.

TWENTY-EIGHT

"Well?" I say later in the dark privacy of the bridge. "Have I gone crazy?"

Captain Redfearn and Mrs. Colding stare at the photo, my phone's glow bathing their faces.

After a moment, they exchange a look.

"What?" I say, heart thumping. "What does that mean?"

"Arie," Mrs. Colding says with great gentleness, "you're forgetting that Evangeline is undead." It takes a moment to sink in. When it does, my head buzzes.

"She has no soul—"

"So why would she show up in a photo?" Mrs. Colding finishes.

My hands clench into white-knuckled fists. "That gaslighting old harpy. How could I be so stupid?"

Captain Redfearn offers a small smile. "She's a manipulator. And you're still new to this world. I wouldn't beat yourself up too much."

I run a hand through my hair, snort out a disbelieving laugh. "*Wow.*" Then, "So what is she up to?"

A dark silence follows.

"It's obvious, isn't?" I continue. "Volok's kept her around all this time as a backup to use against Adrian."

Mrs. Colding and Captain Redfearn trade a look. Clearly, they've been thinking this for some time.

"I mean, it's not like her cover story adds up either," I grumble. "Her? Pushing a mop? *Please*." Captain Redfearn's mouth curves up on one side, but he doesn't say anything.

It sinks in now, making my scalp crawl: the sheer dangerousness of the Commodore. The cunning of that shadowy figure, to send Evangeline against us. To use her to hoover his favorite child back into the fold. The simple genius of it is sickening.

Even from afar, his move was flawless.

At last, Mrs. Colding shifts. "What we *do* know is that it won't do any good telling Adrian. He's not thinking clearly at the moment."

"Which means," I conclude, coming back to myself, "we have to move forward without him. We have to lose this ship following us." I sidle a look at Captain Redfearn. "Any ideas?"

He stands there in the glow of the nav consoles with arms crossed, chin almost to chest. The shape of a yacht glides past in the benighted bay like some immense monster, lights winking.

A deckhand calls out in French. At the stern of a small cabin cruiser nearby, a heavyset man with thinning hair lowers himself into the water, a snorkeling mask in one hand and a serrated diving knife in the other. "Fucking prop again," he hisses.

Captain Redfearn seeing this lifts his head, a rakish smile on his lips. "I just might."

In the pale flush of dawn, I'm on the gangway outside the bridge watching the *Lair* prepare to disembark. The boat hums with an undercurrent of excitement—and also dread. Captain Redfearn stands at the helm beside Mrs. Colding, waiting for the go-ahead. Crew members man the fenders, check for traffic. Then the crew radios crackle: It's time. The captain clanks the anchor back in, and water froths at the stern as the *Lair* glides out to sea.

As predicted, this sets up a buzz of activity on the Nosferyachtu boat. Crew members rush down the gangways, shouting frantically. Their anchor-chain clinks in. My heart lodges in my throat as we begin to turn into the Strait of Bonifacio. *What if the plan doesn't work? What if we can't get a head start on them? What if—*

That's when we hear a nasty, constipated sound. Water churns about the Nosferyachtu boat. The vessel judders and vibrates, listing to the side in a clamoring of angry voices and frantically shifted fenders on neighboring boats. Then a hacking cough—and the engine stalls.

Cries of rage echo in the bay. I can't help but gape. *What the hell did Captain Redfearn do?* Then I notice another witness to this maritime clusterfuck, standing a ways down from me on the shaded gangway: a glaring Evangeline. We lock eyes, and her face slackens. She yanks back a sliding door and stomps inside.

I duck into the bridge with a stupid grin on my face. "What did you do?" I laugh.

Captain Redfearn shrugs as he pilots us safely away into the Strait of Bonifacio. "It's not uncommon for a prop to get fouled by a dock line or tow line." An old sea tar's smirk curls his lips. "Can happen to anyone, really."

And that's when I see the swim fins and snorkeling mask on the seat behind him, still wet. Happiness explodes in my veins. I turn to Mrs. Colding—her cheeks are high in a repressed smile. "You marvelous bastard," I proclaim and lunge forward to plant a kiss on Captain Redfearn's cheek.

I don't know what's more gratifying—his blush or Mrs. Colding's laughter.

We don't waste time. We send a stewardess asking Adrian to join us in the lounge. A rare move. When he arrives, he blinks at the sight of the three of us there, a deep wariness in his face. "Yes?" My hands are clasped tightly before me—a net of butterflies has been set loose in my stomach. Last night I'd come to bed to find him sleeping (or pretending to sleep). I'd curled my fingers in his brambly hair, thinking, *It'd be a lot to take in. Of course he'd be confused. But this will work.*

It has to work.

He'll come back to me.

I glance at Mrs. Colding and Captain Redfearn, and they give me encouraging nods.

I take in a big breath. "You said Evangeline couldn't leave because of the boat following us?"

Adrian lifts a brow.

"Well." I gesture at the miles of empty sea behind us. "It's not following us anymore."

He follows my look and stills, packs of muscle bunching under his suit. His voice, when he speaks, is low and hard with anger. "What did you do?" He eyes Captain Redfearn. "Did you do something?"

My stomach does a little lurch. "I thought you'd be happy—"

"*Did you?*" he repeats, glaring at the captain.

Captain Redfearn flushes but meets his gaze. "I made sure it looked like an accident." Silence blooms in the room like a deadly flower.

"You're kidding me." Adrian's words could cut glass. "Don't you see how dangerous—Jesus Christ, how could you—"

"You should be thanking her for what she did," the captain says.

But Adrian shakes his head, sliding his hands down his face. My teeth unthinkingly go to my lip, sinking in deep to produce a sharp enough pain to keep my tears at bay. This isn't how this was supposed to go.

"You won't tell her to leave?" I ask in a soft voice.

Adrian looks at us all and sighs, smooths an eyebrow with the tips of two fingers. "I . . . I need to think. About next steps."

Next steps.

"I see," I say. "So after Evangeline's little tour of the past last night, suddenly you need to think—"

Adrian's eyes hood, teeth gritted. "I have no interest in this conversation." "No interest in fighting for this relationship, you mean."

He stills as if stabbed in the chest, glances at the captain and chief stew before lifting a finger. "That's not fair."

"Isn't it?" I say, my voice breaking. "Because, if memory serves, I was the one who risked my life to rescue you. And you never even thanked me for it."

Adrian drops his eyes.

"Do you have any idea what I had to go through to do that? And of course Bloodsucking Barbie Bitch comes out of nowhere and—"

He looks down and chuckles, can't help it, and I glare at him. He composes himself and holds up a hand. "You're right, okay? You're right. That was awful of me. Thank you—"

"Do you know what this is doing to me? Do you know how *this*"—I fling a hand at a vase of roses—"makes me feel? Do you have *any* idea, Adrian?"

Adrian's shoulders slump. "I'm sorry—"

"Are you?" I shrill, not caring that my voice is rising, threatening to break up entirely. "Are you really? Because you seem confused lately, Adrian. Do you know what you want anymore?" I swallow and lift a shoulder, trying to reabsorb tears. "Do you want *me?*"

Mrs. Colding looks down, chin trembling. Adrian's face slackens. "Of course I do! How could you say that? I just—"

"Just what, Adrian?"

He swallows, as if poised on that heady brink of saying something one knows may be rash and full of ruinous consequences. When it comes out it's almost a whisper. "I love you, but . . ."

"What?"

"I need some space."

I blink. "What are you saying?"

"I think . . ." Adrian takes in a long breath, holds it. "I think I should move out of the master suite for a bit, into one of the guest cabins. Just until . . . I get some clarity."

My bottom lip is trembling now. I cross my arms tight over my chest. "I see. If you think that's what's best."

Adrian nods, unable to look me in the eyes. Captain Redfearn has turned puce.

But it's Mrs. Colding who moves first.

She turns to Adrian. It is still the same dauntless chief stew, the same withering stare. But there is something new under the flawlessly poised exterior—a nervousness mixed in with a startling volume of cold rage.

She is scared. Scared, and does not care.

"For the record, I do not agree with any of this." Her words are unruffled, deathly quiet. "Arie deserves better."

Adrian is too shocked to say anything. His mouth opens and closes, just like the mouth of a koi fish in a tank.

And she says it. Says words that make me almost burst with pride.

"You should be ashamed of yourself, Adrian."

Adrian blinks as if poleaxed by the swinging boom of a sailing yacht. Then Mrs. Colding has swept out of the room, sucking out all the air with her.

The seconds stretch out, hushed and unbearable. Captain Redfearn looks down, his mouth twitching in what looks suspiciously like a smile. Then he jerks a thumb. "I agree with her." And giving me the briefest of nods, he follows Mrs. Colding.

Leaving just Adrian and me staring at each other across the desolation of the lounge. He tightens his jaw, eyes darting away from me. "I'll get my things—"

"Fuck it," I snap and turn away. "I'll move out myself."

When I decamp down the hall to the door of the first VIP suite, my bundle of stuff hugged to my chest, I freeze and look up.

Evangeline leans on the doorframe of her cabin, arms crossed, watching me. A faint smirk on her lifeless lips.

I throw my stuff inside and slam the door behind me.

TWENTY-NINE

The days somehow continue, trembling with catastrophe as if the *Lair* was up in flames, my life was up in flames, myself a witness with eyes full of fire. What is waiting for me next? What new joyous destruction?

All continues as before. They still chat all day, putting on playful piano performances or lounging on the sun deck to watch the stars. At first, I try to participate. I gamely offer comments and witticisms, and they seem to defer to me, laugh appreciatively. Evangeline goes further; she applauds my slightest of jokes. "How funny Arie is," she'll say with creamy satisfaction. "Isn't she, Adrian?"

I do not know how to handle this. I want to snap at her. I want to slap that infuriating smugness off her face. But I know better now. I know how she operates. My moving out of the master suite had been exactly what she'd wanted, after all. She had known precisely what she was doing. Hadn't she known—I won't put it beyond her—hadn't she known I would follow her and see what I'd seen? That I'd try to do something about it? All this, then, was her testing my relationship with Adrian, and counting on me to stand up for myself and have it blow up in my face.

All according to plan.

So I do not fall into her traps. I do not give in to temptation and dish out sarcastic comebacks. Instead, I hold my drink to my chest and retreat, transform my corner into a high-and-dry spot where I can hold out against the tide, as if what's unfolding before me is nothing but childish comedy.

"Did I mention I've been composing again?" she confides, eyeing Adrian sidelong. "It's a sonata, actually. For you."

I often leave them alone together. I go to the bar for more gin or ice; I go to change into a new outfit or pretend I'm out of sun lotion. On my way down I'll linger just out of sight for a moment, my heart thumping against my ribs. Listening for their voices to change, to drop into a hushed and conspiratorial intimacy. I'll imagine then that Evangeline's long bare toes will creep up Adrian's pants leg. Their hands will roam over each other. They might even dare a risky consummation of tongues. But when I thump back up they are always carefully separated, engaged in some maddeningly ordinary talk. This is their treachery.

How can I think this of Adrian? And how can I not, with the heat of all this fire pressing against my skin?

One day we lie at anchor off the Balearic Islands. Ibiza,

maybe? Mallorca? I don't care. I have to step out onto the deck and get some air; I can't listen to any more of their infuriating chitchat, stomach one more of Adrian's pitying stares. The noonday sun is glancing off the turquoise waters with blinding intensity, and so I have to squint and shade my eyes to make out the tender boat droning toward me.

I know that tender. It belongs to the *Lair*.

And there's a guest seated in the stern, wavy blonde hair whipping in the wind.

My stomach lurches.

I pad down the gangway, hand trailing along the steel rail, eyes never leaving that tender. I'm almost running by the time I skid to a stop and watch Cailee Summers ascend the swim deck staircase like some darling pop star and look about, hands on the hips of her stunning print dress as she takes in the *Lair*. She whips off her oversized cat-eye sunnies and looks right into my face. "I like the new digs," she calls, a devious smirk curling her lips.

I don't remember the next few moments. Not crossing the distance between us or leaping into her arms. All I know is, all my worries have dropped away and we're jumping up and down and shrieking with laughter, tears in our eyes. "What are you *doing* here?" I squeal.

She shrugs a flirtatious shoulder. "Apparently your billionaire boyfriend was worried about you, so he flew me down here." She brushes at her hair with a melodramatic flourish. "It seems word of my legendary pep talks has spread."

I glance back at the main salon. Adrian stands in the doorway, hands in pockets, smiling at us.

Heat rushes into my cheeks as I mouth the words: *Thank you.*

After our little celebratory dance is over, I have the first mate extend the swim platform out from the stern of the *Lair* so we can have some privacy. Cailee tongues the corner of her mouth as she watches him work. "How you ever concentrate around here, I will never know," she muses, and I have to laugh and drag her past, linking my arm in hers. "You're insufferable." We lie out in the sun in bikinis, sunglasses on, as the platform bobs gently on the waves. I can't remember the last time the sun felt this good.

As usual, Cailee gets right down to business.

"Spill it," she orders. "What's going on?"

For all the heat on my skin, I feel a prickling chill on it and twist around to see what I'm expecting to see.

Evangeline, watching us from the shade of the bridge deck awning. I shiver.

Cailee rolls onto her tummy to look too. She pulls her sunnies down her nose to fix me with a dry look. "Is that . . .?"

"His wife? Yup." I flop back onto my towel and huff out a sigh. "Back from the dead, you could say."

Cailee's jaw drops. "You're *shitting* me."

I shake my head.

"And you're still *here?*"

I tingle all over with a blush. "It's a long story. She's—*here* for a little bit."

"But—"

"Ugh, I don't wanna talk about it," I groan, one hand on my forehead as I make a hurry up motion with the other. "What's been going on with you?"

Cailee gives me a look before flopping onto her back again. She draws her legs up and folds her hands on her stomach, assuming a matter-of-fact tone. "Oh, not much. Just trying to figure out my life after you exiled me from the yachting industry without, you know, a *word* of explanation."

I peek a look at her, eyes squinted in a wince under my shades. "Sorry."

She returns the look, letting me dangle before rolling her eyes. "Anyway, it's why I can only stay the day. Got some stuff lined up back in Florida."

I arch a brow. "Oh?"

She smirks. "I'm not tellin' *you*, Miss Mysterious," she says, pushing my face away. "You'll find out soon enough."

I bark a laugh. It almost instantly makes me want to cry.

She doesn't have to look at me to know what I'm going through. Her eyes watch the blue, blue sky. The waves lap against the fiberglass shell of the platform. "It feels like forever ago that we were both in Florida, and you got that call from Lair Yachting Incorporated. Now look at you."

I don't respond. My throat has swelled shut.

"Do you know what you're gonna do?"

I bite my lip to stop the sting of tears in my nostrils. "No idea."

She takes a minute to think on it. "If it was *me*," she says at last with only a dollop of insinuation, "I'd make his ass prove he loves me."

I suck in a choked laugh. "How?"

She shrugs. "Find a way to test him."

I look over at her. Her slithery, unpredictable yet calming energy. The upturned impishness of her lips. I grip her hand. "I'm glad you're here," I whisper.

She turns her head and rests her cheek on the towel to look at me, those wry lips curving in a smile. "Me too."

I don't even care that I can still feel Evangeline's eyes on my skin.

We spend the rest of the afternoon lolling on the platform or staging ridiculous selfies for Cailee on various parts of the *Lair*. "Hashtag yachtie hottie!" she calls on the forward sunbeds, legs spread and lips pouted like a porn star. "Ow, ow, ow!" I crack up and shake my head.

I can't stop the day from slipping away, though, and before long night has fallen on the Mediterranean and the tender is readied again.

We say goodbye in the mouth of the beach club by the swim deck. Tears push into my eyes, and my throat is too ragged with emotion to say anything. She makes a sympathetic face and gathers me into her arms. "Don't wait two months to call me next time."

I nod.

She steps back and looks past me. Adrian is there, with Evangeline and Mrs. Colding beside him. Cailee nods at him. "Thank you for the invitation, Mr. Voper."

He nods, his eyes sliding to me, gauging my mood. "Anytime."

Cailee goes still as Evangeline steps forward and takes her hands, dialing up the charm. "I wish we'd had time to get to know each other, Cailee."

Cailee's smile doesn't reach her eyes. "That makes one of us." She looks Evangeline up and down. "I know a viper when I see one."

My jaw drops in an astonished gush of admiration. Evangeline's face slackens.

Cailee winks at me, and with that she's strutting out onto the swim deck, letting the first mate offer his hand and help her aboard. "Why thank you," she purrs, and I have to grin, knowing that mate will be late getting back.

Evangeline, lip snarling, sweeps back into the *Lair*, and Adrian tosses me a conflicted look before going after her.

But I am not alone. Mrs. Colding stands beside me, watching the tender skim across the moonlit waves toward the glimmering lights of Ibiza. "I like her," she says, and I snort.

"I do, too."

But my smile fades as I think back on what she said.

THIRTY

My high from Cailee's visit lasts only a day or two. When I begin to drink again, it's more than I ever have—I can't stop thinking about what she said. What used to be two drinks in the evenings turns to three or four, and I'm putting more gin in them. Sometimes it's still day out when I start. A few times Mrs. Colding and Captain Redfearn approach me, asking what's next. *"Arie, we have to talk. What's our plan for going after the Commodore?"* But I brush them off as they trade sad, sympathetic looks. Can't they see what's happening to my world?

The gin is poured earlier and earlier in the day.

Today is one of those days.

I study Evangeline through bleary eyes as she chats with Adrian on the top deck, my third cocktail of the day cradled against my chest. I've flung my thoughts back to her suite. What I saw. That wardrobe looking like a crime scene. It doesn't fit. How can this woman be the same strict and fanatical woman I'd heard about from Mrs. Colding? There is nothing in that wardrobe I can relate to the figure in those stories.

A word surfaces in my mind: *Liar*. And another: *Fraud*.

Of course. Unless it was all for show. That squeaky clean main room that could be seen by anyone from the hall? A performance. It was all a performance. The roses, the piano playing, the serious and unsmiling attention to orderliness? All an act for Adrian, to remind him of who he had fallen in love with, no matter that person was long gone. That wardrobe was the truth—the rotten self beneath. This woman laughing now with Adrian? An impostor. A slick operator, slathering makeup over a crude imitation. Which would mean—it hits me now in a blast of mirth—they were both trying so very hard to love people they no longer were.

A joke.

I snort into my glass, and Adrian lofts an eyebrow at me.

"Sorry." I lift a hand. "Sorry." *Wow*, this gin is really getting to me. *It's just a freaking closet, Arie.* For Chrissake, it's ridiculous I'm coming to these conclusions. But I don't care. Closet or no, it's all I have to hold on to. Otherwise, the alternative—the unspeakable alternative—is too much to bear.

I can't help it. I snort again, shoulders hunched to repress the giggles, and clap a hand over my mouth. Adrian and Evangeline exchange a look.

"Welp," I declare, shaking the ice in my glass. "Out again." I struggle up and bump into the wet bar, giggling. "Whoopsy."

Adrian's eyes hood. "Don't you think you've had enough?"

The gin glugs loudly into the glass. I don't bother with the tonic. "Enough to listen to her?" I wave a hand. "Pffft."

Evangeline rolls her eyes. Adrian's face has hardened. "Aurora. You're being rude."

"Oh, I'm sorry, was I interrupting your little heart-to-heart?"

Evangeline lays a hand on Adrian's arm. "I'm interrupting. I should go." She rises, and Adrian sighs. "Ev . . ."

"Oh *no*," I groan in a mock plaintive tone. "Don't go, Ev!"

Evangeline touches Adrian's wrist as she passes him. "If you want to hang out later, feel free to drop by." One last blank look at me over her shoulder, and she's sweeping down the stairs— poised, serene, secure in her wifely role. A star.

When she's gone, Adrian looks at me. "Happy now?"

I nod, gulping back gin. "Very."

He shakes his head and rises. "Do you have to make a scene?"

"It seems to be the only way to get your attention these days."

His scowl lasts only for a moment: I stumble and he catches my arm, but I jerk it away. "Donneed your help," I slur, and when I lift my glass to drink I stagger again and Adrian catches me, removing the glass from my hand and setting it on the bartop. "I think you're done."

"No!"

"Come on. Let's get you to bed."

I'm not a great walking partner. Before I know it, he's swept me up in his arms and is carrying me down to my suite. I curl my fingers against his shirt and breathe in his scent, remembering when he carried me abovedeck, only a few months ago, to show me the Northern Lights.

How pathetic, that this is the only way I can get intimacy from him now.

"Lemme down," I snap, heavy with a sudden, confusing anger. Adrian objects, but I've already twisted out of his arms. I stagger to the bed and collapse onto it.

"Come on," he says, trying for a jocular tone. "Scootch over."

When I roll over to give him room, he sits on the edge of the bed and looks down at me, his dark face a mystery against the light. Maybe it always has been.

But that's not true. I know that expression, rare as it is.

I know when he's consumed with guilt.

"I don't like seeing you like this," he whispers, and I can't argue. I don't like it either. Drinking, sneaking, envying—this is not me. What have I become?

Adrian brushes the hair back from my brow, and maybe it's the tenderness in that gesture—the feeling of receptiveness or vulnerability—that makes me say it.

"Then fix it."

It accomplishes what I feared. The withdrawing of the hand, the wounded closing up of his features.

I can still hurt him, after all.

I look away. "You should go. She's waiting for you."

His reply is an incredulous expulsion of breath. "*What?*"

"She clearly wanted you to go to her room." And then I say the words that neither of us will ever forget: "Haven't you already?"

The room hums. Adrian's mouth works. "Aurora—"

"A man shouldn't neglect his wife."

The invocation of this word changes everything. His face slams down like a steel gate. "Look—"

"Go." I roll away from him. When he doesn't move, I shout it. "*Go!*"

He sits there for a long moment not saying anything, lips peeled back tight against his teeth.

When he finally gets up, he shudders as if—even dead—he has a chill.

When the door clicks shut, I get out of bed and pace about with one hand pressed to my stomach, taking noisy breaths. *I did it,* I think to myself. *Oh God, I've done it. What have I done?* I pick up a shirt of his and smell it, seeing if I can detect her scent on it. I cram it into my mouth, as much to stop the howls as the scenes from rising up in my head. The scenes of what could be happening in that guest cabin right now.

Such excruciating pain, at the thought of his hands on her. Will she bring out in him a passion I have never seen before? The next time he makes love to me, will it be different, clearly intended to satisfy the wants, the particularities, of someone else?

Will he call her his Northern Light?

I can't do it. I can't keep away. I open the door and pad down the hall to that other door. It's invitingly ajar, as if waiting for me. Waiting for me to see.

I peer through the crack.

They're not in bed together. They stand facing each other, she in a suggestive babydoll, he with his hands on his hips. He's shaking his head as she speaks in a low, earnest tone, speaks words straight out of my nightmares. "Why stay with her? You know it won't end well."

"Don't say that."

"You know it's true."

I hold my breath, my skin buzzing with a sure sense of betrayal.

"You'll never find Volok. You'll always be what you are now. Which means you will watch her die. Why have a fleeting love with her when we could have ours forever?"

Adrian sucks in a long, shuddering breath and covers his eyes with a hand. "I—I don't want to be this anymore. She—"

"Is a girl you just met. I was the love of your life, Adrian. I'm your *wife*. And I'm back now." She steps forward and lifts her long, pallid hands to cradle his face. "So why are we even talking about this?"

Adrian is still staring into her eyes—caught—when I tear myself away. I have to put an arm across my mouth and bite it, bite my flesh, to stop the pain. To stop the howl of protest I'm afraid will come out of me and never stop coming.

I did it. It's happened. I made the worst thing happen. I couldn't trust him and pushed him away.

Back in my suite I grope for the whiskey bottle in the liquor cabinet, its lip chattering against the rim of the glass as I pour. I think of what's to become of me next. Perhaps they'll sit me down tomorrow and explain to me the situation. They've been reunited. Their love never truly went away. What else was to be expected? It is time for me to leave. And perhaps I would leave, stepping off the bow and letting the water take me, gulping it down (I gulp my whiskey), a romantic act that one only reads about in very old stories. Or perhaps they'd invite me to stay on the boat, wanting to be friends. They would keep me on out of pity and invite me to join them in the evenings, and I'd be grateful even for this humiliation.

No. I'd be dead to them. They would drop me off at some port and I'd never see them again.

Would I ask Adrian to bite me, so I could be with him? Would he still choose her then?

I drink my whiskey. The burning fire of it seems fresh and restorative to me, like water from a mountain spring. I gulp it down.

Perhaps this is what it tastes like. Perhaps this is what Adrian and Evangeline taste, when they taste what's inside us all.

THIRTY-ONE

In the morning I watch to see if their behavior has changed. Will they be unable to hide their feelings? Will their cold self-possession break, revealing giggling and maddening displays of affection? Or will they continue their treacherous performance, their sly averted looks, until I have to claw and scratch at them, scream until my throat bursts, to get it out of them? What new horrors will be waiting for me?

But I needn't have worried, for what I see is far from any of that. It is unmistakable: There is a distance between them. Evangeline looks diminished and worried. Adrian for his part avoids her—avoids both of us—going off for long walks about the boat on his own, hands in pockets and head bowed. A few times Evangeline approaches him with hushed, conciliatory words, but he fends her off and my heart sings.

Maybe they didn't sleep together. She overstepped her bounds and pushed him away.

He's come to his senses.

This brings up in me a softness, a sweet devotion, girlish and pure. All I have to do is wait for him, then. He will come sooner or later.

I go into port to shop. I walk amongst the other tourists in the dazzling sea-light, the other people with their untold stories kept within themselves. I buy a pistachio gelato and idly lick it while I take in the brightly colored stucco houses, the boutiques selling sunglasses and postcards and rope sandals. The mild air, the laughter, the flat-roofed architecture with its simple cheerfulness, all seems part of a fluid, peaceful light-heartedness that urges me to have faith, to revel in the present. And I am. I *am* light-hearted. I am weightless and flooded with light, the warmth of the sun on my face, another thing that Evangeline cannot have. I have to repeat it in my head, to reassure myself of its reality: *She struck out. She lost.*

I finish my gelato with great relish.

The street stalls are chockablock with racks of trendy clothing. I pick through them, wondering what Adrian would like to see me in, and end up buying a flouncy flower-print dress hued in warm marigold. Gold, to bring out the yellow in my green eyes. He likes my eyes.

When I return to the *Lair* shining at the pier, I wait in my suite on the edge of the bed, the modest skirt with its innocent ruffles carefully arranged about me. I clasp my hands just so in my lap. I put on a bright smile.

The hours pass.

It does not occur to me that he won't come. The belief in his coming is so sure it is like a belief in the sun. And so the light has begun to fade behind the window curtains when it at last hits me: *He's not coming.*

My eyes fill with tears. I take off the dress, slowly and ceremoniously, and hang it in the closet.

Then I lie down in bed in my pajamas and order room service. I ask for another bottle of whiskey.

I fall asleep early. I leave the whiskey bottle, half-empty, lying on its side on the rug by the bed, my cheek mashed into my pillow. I have never welcomed sleep more.

It's three in the morning when the door to my suite creaks open.

It takes me a moment to comprehend it. I'm still groggy from the whiskey, my head doing its damnedest to split itself open. I have to blink to make out the shadow standing there in the dark. Tall, shapely, with molded waves of hair. Where the eyes should be is a shimmer of white.

"Hello, Arie," Evangeline says.

I scramble up against the headboard, my heart pounding in my ribcage.

"What are you—what do you want?"

She flows into the room. I glimpse curves of flesh in the faint moonlight that's streaming through the window curtains. She's wearing some sort of negligee. It shines like fish scales—like a ghost—in the dark, champagne-colored and sheer with a neckline that dives down her front. It seems as if her body is about to slip out of it at any moment, signifying its appetite and availability.

"I think we got off on the wrong foot," she says.

It's hard not to laugh at this.

"No," I reply. "I think we both know exactly who the other is."

If she's offended by this, she takes it in stride. She is full of boundless understanding. "I don't know why we should treat each other like enemies. We both want what's best for Adrian, don't we?"

"You will never be what's best for him," I spit.

This is harder to swallow. Her dark face tightens, then smooths over again. "I think we can agree we both make him happy."

I look away, breathing hard through my nose.

There's a sly little smile on her face now. I can see it gleaming in the dark as she flows closer. "But at the moment he's not happy. The fact that he can only have one of us is torturing him." Her eyes drop, pointedly. She's toeing the whiskey bottle with one long, bare foot. "And not only him, it appears."

The heat now, rushing into my cheeks. My brow. My ears. Suddenly, I am very aware of how close she is to the bed. "What are you saying?"

She looks at me out of eyes full of kindness or pity or something far stranger and accommodating. Then she reaches up and slips her negligee off her frail shoulders, letting it pool in a silky puddle of light at her feet. "There's a way for all of us to be together, Arie."

My tongue cleaves to the roof of my mouth. I feel sick, light-headed, fluttery, and just a little bit aroused. I force myself to look away from her sex.

"What are you—"

But she's bending down over the bed now, crawling onto it, the sweet drooping of her breasts causing the blood to hammer through my veins. I shrink back.

"I've seen you watching me," she breathes in a husky sigh.

"What? No, I—"

"I've been watching you, too. Did you think Adrian's the only one who appreciates your body?"

A hot flush floods my face. I don't know where to look. I have to try hard—very hard—to ignore what my body is telling me. To what her words are doing to my body.

"Do you think it was lost on me, that your little sunbathing performance was also for my benefit?" She's slipping under the covers with me, her shadowed face close. I can see her tongue moisten her plump lips. I can see her eyes. "I know what you want."

I shake my head, as in a trance. "I want Adrian," I whisper.

"Then have him," she breathes, and kisses me.

I've never kissed a woman's lips before. They are smooth, supple, delicious. Blood flows to all the dry places in my body, leaving me dizzy. The room vibrates, the walls suddenly very far away. I think I might faint.

At last, I pull away. "I can't."

"Why not?" She is inches from me, studying my lips. "I can tell you've been abused. It takes a victim to know another."

So that's what she's been hiding.

"I can't tell you how comfortable it feels—how *good* it feels—to be with a woman." And she reaches down and places her hand, very firmly, against the silk pajamas between my legs. "Let me show you."

I suck in a breath and grip her wrist, but do not remove it. I am, to my shame, very wet.

Her hand begins to move, with a brisk determined passion, between my legs. I rest my brow on hers. I shake my head. "This is wrong."

"No," she sighs. "This is love."

Her hand continues its quick, secret work. She presses herself against me. I can feel her hard nipples against my chest. "Think of it: the three of us, sharing our love. Love can be whatever you want it to be, Arie. Wouldn't this be better than nothing at all?" She is kissing me, on my cheeks, my brow, my jaw. She is everywhere, her heavy scent curling into my nostrils. Her cajoling reasoning fills my ears.

Wouldn't it be better? A bearable compromise, in order to stay with Adrian? And who knows what I might discover with a woman in bed. A safety I'd never known with a man. Perhaps in time I'd come to prefer her over him. Her love—safe, female, mysterious—over his.

I can feel my sense of self slipping. I can feel it happening—the waiting shadows thickening and closing in, pressing up against me, all the way up into the high corners of the room.

"Please," I beg.

"Just give in," she breathes against my skin, and touches the tip of her tongue, the pricks of two long, curved teeth, to my neck.

My eyes snap open.

She must not expect it, for my explosive push dumps her out of the bed. "Get away from me!" I hiss. My skin is crawling. Tears—confoundingly—have sprung to my eyes. I wipe at my arms as if slapping away spiders. "Get away from me. Oh God, get away from me. *Get away from me!*"

She rises from the floor like a liquid accumulation of malice. Eyes blazing, shoulders ridged up like a cat's, her incisors snicked out sharp and bright in the moonlight. "You ungrateful *bitch*," she spits, and my heart stops in my chest. "I'm offering you more than you ever deserve, and you're throwing it away?" She shakes her head, a wild sneer twisting those pillowy lips, and looks me up and down. "This is ridiculous. I could take you now—"

I somehow get it out: "And Adrian would hate you forever."

She freezes, and for the first time I see fear flicker across her perfect face. Her taloned hands curl into claws at her sides. I cannot breathe. There's an ill sweat, cool and damp, on my brow and chest, trickling down my ribs under my arms. And I think, *What will I taste like?*

Then she's snarled and flowed backward out of the room without a sound, her white flesh dissolving into the shadows. I stare at the dark space where she used to be for a long time, my heart pistoning in my chest, the terror like a fever in my brain. Then I snap. I lunge out of bed and stumbling and falling on rubber legs I lock the door behind her and slide down against it, sobbing out a grief I do not understand.

"Don't be ridiculous," Adrian says. "She would never do that."

I've found him before first light and dragged him into the master suite. He shakes his head as I tell him. "I'm telling you, she tried to seduce me. Adrian, I"—I drop my voice, glancing through the open door down the hall—"I don't know why she came back, but it's not for you. There's some other agenda here. She was going to *bite me*, Adrian."

He scoffs. "You've been drinking. You got confused."

I give him a flat look, thinking, *And I haven't even told you the half of it.* "I spent the night barricaded in my cabin. Don't tell me what did and did not happen."

He sighs. "Okay, I'm sorry—"

I point a finger as I pace. "Your wife is a fucking piece of work, Adrian. I mean, *goddamn*, you almost have to admire it."

"Look, it must've been a misunderstanding—"

I stop in my tracks. "You really don't believe me, do you?" I snort out an incredulous laugh. "You don't believe me."

"Aurora—"

"*Wow.*" I pace again, one hand to my forehead, and turn to him. "Okay, fine. You want to know the truth? You want to finally hear it? She threatened to murder me, Adrian."

He looks away. "Jesus."

"And back at Voper Manor," I go on, voice rising over his, "I saw her meet with someone from the Nosferyachtu Club." I let that sink in. "She's working for them, Adrian. She's working for Volok."

He lets his chin fall to his chest, his voice a groan. "Aurora . . ."

"I know. I know you don't want to hear it. You want to believe she's the same woman you married all those years ago. But we both know she's changed. Whatever you loved before— whatever you fell in love with—she's no longer that, is she?" He can't say anything to this, and I know. I know it's true.

So I ask it. "Do you love me?"

He looks at me, eyes haunted. "Yes."

"Do you still love her?"

He looks down, lids pinched shut. The words, when they come, are pained, exhausted, barely above a whisper. Blood from a stone. "I don't know."

It's an act of will to keep standing, to stop my heart from dropping out of my chest.

I see. I see.

I back away, eyes glassing up. He looks at me with profound regret. "Baby . . ."

But I can't. I can't hear that right now. If he says it again, I might scream. "I won't bother you anymore," I find myself saying. "I'll let you make your choice."

And I leave him standing there in the master suite, looking like a man whose purpose has been stripped from him.

THIRTY-TWO

I fantasize about Evangeline's demise.

And not just her being found out and slinking off the boat, humbled and disgraced, brought down to size. I think of pushing her into the hot sun and watching her turn into something beautiful, rapturous with fire, shriveled and diminished. I think of her arms and legs wrenched away, her head torn off. Exquisite vengeance. I think of staking her heart and watching a foul, black, venomous substance spurt out, leaking away and depriving her of whatever dreadful lifeforce that had animated her. *How dare you,* I would tell her as I watched her suffer. I would lean in and show her my teeth in a little, satisfied and gloating smile, and I would say it. *Not my man. Not my man.*

This is who I could become when defending Adrian.

But this is all nonsense, of course. That kind of sweet justice is a fairy tale. What's more likely is her flowing into this room, pouring through the keyhole like a mist, stealing over my bed in a hush of inimical temptation. She must get rid of the evidence, after all. I know what she is now. What she is capable of. These are the fairy tales that endure—because they're true.

Such are my thoughts as I huddle in bed. The door locked, curtains drawn. I've been here for days now, watching mindless TV shows or lying flopped out on my back, staring at the ceiling. The ironic symmetry of my life brings up in me a sickening urge to laugh. Once, I was imprisoned in a cabin on the *Lair* against my will, like some heroine in a gothic romance. And here I am now, imprisoned again, but this time of my own free will. I believe there is some important message in that, but I don't know what it is.

On the second day Adrian comes to the door, pleading with me to come out and talk. But I don't respond. It's a long time—a heart-squeezingly long time—before he gives up and leaves.

On the third day Evangeline comes.

I can see her shadow in the crack of light under the door. Her dulcet voice floats through that crack, raising the hairs on the back of my neck.

Arie. Open the door.

No.

This is all a misunderstanding. Why don't you come out so I can explain myself?

Does Adrian know she's here? Is he there, by her side, a silent accomplice? Or did she sneak down here without his knowing?

You know you want to. I know you think of me.

The feel of her flesh against mine. Her hand on my sex, her teeth grazing my neck, dizzying in its intoxication.

I know you want me.

I press a hand over my mouth, feeling a traitorous throbbing between my legs. *We can still have that love.*

I slide down under the covers and put my hands over my ears, blocking out the dripping poison of her words. Lord help me, this woman. This woman.

Arie.

The doorknob jiggles.

Don't make me angry.

Oh God.

Arie . . .

Someone help me . . .

"Arie?"

I jerk out of a noxious fog of sleep. I'm in bed, the sheets pulled over my head. I claw them away and sit up.

A knock. Someone knocking at the door. I was having a dream.

Or was I?

"Who is it?" I call, threatening.

The reply is simple, unvarnished, patient. "It's me, dear." I know that voice.

When I unlock the door, I barely give the dark figure in the hallway a glance. By the time Mrs. Colding has stepped inside and I've growled at her to lock the door behind her, I'm already back in bed and curled up in a ball, facing the wall.

Mrs. Colding sighs, and I know she's studying the empty liquor bottles scattered about the stateroom.

"I can see why the stewardesses are afraid to come in here," she quips.

Ha-ha. Mrs. Colding made a joke.

Another sigh, and then she's sitting on the bed. When I don't turn over, she says it. "Look at me, dear." I groan, but give in. Her face is set in a calm, practical, determined way, her hands folded in her lap. "This won't do anymore."

I shrug.

"What's your plan?"

"What do you mean?"

"You know what I mean."

Another shrug. "Whatever makes him happy." And I turn away.

I can hear her breathing through her nose. She's angry—or disappointed?—but controlling it. She brushes at something on her skirt. "You once asked me about my husband."

I lie there, the blood drumming in my ears.

"You still want to know what happened?"

After a moment, I nod.

I can hear her breathe in, as if gathering herself. Her voice affects that light and carefully detached tone it does when relaying a story, as if the past were something to be treated with great respect.

Tread carefully. Here be dragons.

"I was young," she begins. "Too young, really. My father pressured me into the marriage. I didn't know the man, but I felt rescued from insignificance, buoyed up by his gallantry. I was a Chinese girl, after all. Bound not only by the deep traditions of that culture, but by the rules every woman knows, which are reasonless and absolute. Shouldn't I be grateful?"

I lie very still, hushed and trembling. I cannot recognize the woman who is speaking now, cannot believe Mrs. Colding could ever have been like that—like me.

I listen closely. I desire revelations.

But she continues haltingly. Her mouth forms a wistful line. "It wasn't until I came to live with him that I discovered how dangerous he was."

My skin grows cold. "So your husband, he wasn't the one you loved . . ."

She shakes her head. "That came later, with the servant boy." She laughs, a low, broken sound. "He really was just a boy. But he saved me. We saved each other. He was poor, like I had been, and gentle. And when my husband found out . . ."

My insides clench.

"He showed me. On the eve of a trip for our wedding anniversary, he showed me what he'd done to my Miguel . . ." Her voice cracks and I sit up, heart pounding, and slip my hand into hers. She holds it very tight. "Something inside me shut down that day. Became cold and hard." Her eyes fall. "But it wasn't enough for my husband. He began to take his vengeance on me. And that's when Adrian intervened."

Adrian?

"He happened to be docked there that night. After he . . ." She pauses, her throat bobbing in a swallow. "After he was done feeding, we talked. He offered me a position aboard his boat. He gave me purpose, a sense of belonging. I will forever be grateful for that. But now I see." Her lips curl inward in self-reproach. "I closed myself off. Not just to life, but to the very notion of romance. I was not going to allow a man to treat me like that again. Instead, I devoted myself to saving Adrian, not realizing I was trading one abusive relationship for another." She looks at me. "Then you came along. And you stood up to him. I would never have been able to do that myself before I saw that. I have never admired anyone more."

Admired. Her. Mrs. Colding. Admires *me*.

I blink back tears, my spirits hushed and dizzied as she shakes my hand.

"You've shown me it can work. That it's worth trying for. So when this is over, I'm going to try again. Captain Redfearn . . ." Spots of red appear in her cheeks, and for a moment I glimpse the young woman she once had been.

"*No!*" I gasp. "Captain *Redfearn?*"

Her blush deepens, and she nods. "He's made his feelings clear. He's been patient, waiting for me. I think—I think it's time." She grips both my hands now, staring directly into my eyes. "What I'm saying, dear—what I'm trying to say—is don't stop fighting for yourself."

Sudden vertigo takes me. My lip trembles.

"Do you hear?" she says. "Promise me. Never stop fighting."

I nod helplessly and fling myself at her, arms tight around her neck. "Thank you," I whisper into her ear, and then I cannot speak for the longest time. It takes everything I have to keep the sobs from wrecking me.

She must be surprised. She is rigid for a moment, and then she lifts her arms and, with utmost caution and tenderness, wraps them about me, as if she has forgotten how to do such a thing. And even more strange, her chest swells as if holding something in, and then her shoulders hitch, her fingers clutch into my shirt. When I pull back to look, tears glisten in bright tracks down her cheeks.

Mrs. Colding is crying.

We look into each other's faces and laugh, helpless, like a pair of sisters. Then she turns away and wipes at her cheeks, composing herself. "Well," she says and rises, smoothing her skirt. "I'm going to do some snooping around. I don't trust that—what did you call her?"

I laugh. "Bloodsucking Barbie Bitch."

She points a finger. "*That*. I don't trust her for a second. So, I'm going to find some evidence that proves to Adrian she's working for the Commodore."

"Her phone," I say, remembering. "She has a phone in her room. In a safe in the walk-in wardrobe. If there's any dirt to be found on her, it'd be on that."

Her mouth downturns and she nods, filing that away. Then she cups my chin and studies me as if reassuring herself of some rare and pleasing constant in the world. I hold very still.

Her eyes twinkle, and she lightly squeezes. "Consider it done," she says at last. "Then we're going to chuck her over the side with Adrian's blessing, and get back to hunting. All right?" She waits for my nod. Then her lips pert in that mysterious way of theirs and she slips out the door.

I lie back on the bed and stare up at the ceiling, trying to breathe around the terrifying lightness in my chest.

THIRTY-THREE

I break my self-imposed exile as night is falling.

It's as if something immense and long-dormant inside me shifts, answering some inscrutable summons. I need light and air; I cannot think without it. I throw back the curtains to the suite's expansive windows and squint at the twinkling contours of pure whiteness that greets me. Snow. A wall of icepack glides past my window. Where the hell am I?

I need to go abovedeck and see.

I bundle myself up into a fur-fringed parka and unlock the door and crack it open, poke my head out into the hall. Nothing. No slinky, lurking shadows. No Evangeline.

I slide one foot out into the hall, tentatively, as if edging out onto the ice of a pond that may or may not be safely frozen over. Then wait, listening, eyeing both ends of the hall. My heart pounds in my ribs. My breath hangs in my throat. The *Lair*, suddenly, has the feel of a haunted ship.

Where will she be waiting for me? Will I scream if I see her? Will I have time to?

Will anybody hear me if I do?

I'm shaking as I pad to the spiral staircase that'll take me abovedeck.

But it's my thoughts, not Evangeline, that catch up to me as I hurry up the steps. I've been avoiding it, I know. Thinking about what Mrs. Colding told me. The import of it. *Don't stop fighting for yourself.* Because I know what that means. What she had in her indirect way been getting at.

You have to trust in a relationship, but there's a line. I have thrown myself into doubts and agonies, thinking I was unfair for not trusting Adrian enough. But I've reached that line. If he cannot choose—*will not choose*—I'll have to choose for him.

I'll have to walk away.

A deep and furious refusal meets this. How could I think this way? How could I not? Perhaps it was something that had to do with my outlook on love. Ordinary love, ordinary affection, was not enough. It was something that had to be painful beyond bearing, beyond hope, to give it meaning. To make it true. But perhaps—perhaps—that was not true. That was a fiction I have told myself all these years to get through the horrific bumps and dry patches of life.

(This is worthwhile. This pain has meaning.)

I have a dramatic notion of getting down on my knees. *This,* I think to myself. *This is important.*

I have come to the edge. Where the questions you've been afraid to ask yourself—the questions that have lain in wait sharpening themselves like knives—press now into the ribs, deep into the heart.

(How long will I bear this? Do I have to bear this?)

(No.)

The unwelcome revelation. That my journey to save Adrian has taken me so far, and the last step now would be to step beyond him, where he cannot go, and continue on without him.

That I'd only been fooling myself into believing I'd changed if I didn't stand up for myself now and do what has to be done.

When I step out onto the main deck, I find I'm freezing and hug myself in my parka. Why is it so goddamn cold? I'm so lost in my thoughts that I'm nearing the bow of the boat when I look up and the blood drains from my face.

All about me a cold sea stretches, broken up by floating icebergs, scalloped whorls of ice glowing like unearthly sculptures in the hushed and eerie twilight. And in the bemirrored calm of the water, a whorling of eerie green, shimmering like a mirage. A reflection of what's above in the sky.

The Northern Lights.

It happens slowly, like an oncoming fever: a prickling of rage, tickling and itching my scalp, my cheeks, down my arms, growing in power as I stare up at those petty-dancers flaring overhead.

When I hear the footstep, I know. I know he's behind me.

My teeth grind.

"How could you?" My breath pants out in a fog of misery in the arctic air. I am one solid accusation. "I can't believe you'd bring me here with *her* onboard."

But he does not speak. Somewhere, far away, an iceberg cracks and groans in the silence.

A sudden brimming of tears blinds me.

"I can't do this anymore, Adrian," I whisper. "I can't keep trusting you if you can't—" I look down, my lip betraying me, beginning to tremble. I bite it. "So I've made a choice. I don't deserve this. I refuse to be treated this way." I turn about, my whole body locked and hands clenched in righteous fury. "So if you don't see how lucky—"

But the words catch in my throat, because he's not standing behind me. No. Adrian Voper, his face aching and nervous and pure as snow, is not standing. He's on bended knee. And something I cannot understand is happening. He's holding a little black box before me, and it's open, something flashing out of it. A diamond. A ring. An engagement ring.

Adrian Voper is proposing to me.

The world quivers. "What . . ." I breathe.

"Aurora Strand," he says, and my heart swells in my chest at the formality of that address. What it means.

No. This can't be happening.

"You're the best thing in my life. The best thing that's ever happened to me. And I've been an idiot."

A horrifying laugh slips out of me. I nod, blinded with tears. "Yes. Yes, you have."

"I'm so sorry for putting you through that. You *do* deserve better. And you've stood by me through all of it. If there's any way you can forgive me, I'll prove to you I can be a better man." His face tightens as he hesitates. "When she came back . . ." The words tremble with self-loathing, and he swallows. "It made me question everything. Maybe, even, whether or not I wanted to go through with freeing myself." His eyes flick away in shame, the muscles in his sharp jaw flashing like minnows in the water, and he meets my gaze again.

"But you were right. You were always right. She's not who she used to be. And even if she was, it wouldn't have mattered. I was infatuated with an illusion. I was in love with an idea of who I was before I became *this*, indulging her out of some twisted sense of marital obligation, while she tried to turn me into what she had become. Whereas you . . ." The line of his mouth crooks up in a wondering smile. "I'm who I want to be when I'm around you, Aurora. You're my Northern Light. You fight for my best self, not my worst. You make me *me*. I never thought I'd feel that again." His eyes glass up, his voice growing hoarse. "And the thought of losing that—of losing *you*—I wouldn't be able to bear that, Aurora. Not that."

I hold a hand to my chest. My heart wants to pound out of it. There's a ringing in my ears.

Please keep talking, I think.

He settles his shoulders, hands tightly gripping the velvet ring box. "So I told her. It's done. She's leaving the boat now—a helicopter is coming to pick her up. And I took you here so I could ask what your father asked your mother under the Northern Lights." He straightens his spine. "So." And his face lights up in that brilliant smile of his I can never get used to. "Aurora Strand," he says, "will you marry me?"

It almost knocks me over, the size and power of it. The happiness. This is immediately followed by a springing pressure of tears. My laugh is cracked and disbelieving, and he laughs as he stares into my eyes. "You mean it?" I say, holding a hand to my mouth.

Yes, he says with his eyes, nodding. *Yes. I do.*

I hold his face, his skin like frost, and press my lips to his in a series of tender, mewling kisses, hiccupping laughs as we rest our foreheads together. His vivid blue eyes lock with mine. "Yes?" he asks, and I nod.

"Yes," I manage back in a thick voice, laughing. "Yes, yes, yes . . ." The sickening knot of betrayal and accusation in me loosens, setting me aglow. I have been wiped clean, borne up, freed.

Now he is sliding the ring onto my finger, snug and secure, a perfect fit. The sight of it there steals my breath away, causing a succession of fluttery quivers to overtake me. It's surreal, and yet somehow so instantly *right*. And then he is holding me, he has caught me up in his arms and is kissing me under that dazzling northshine, dispelling all my forlorn vapors in a blinding swirl of happiness as he whirls me about, laughing, folding me in. Together. Us again.

Us.

THIRTY-FOUR

We hold hands as we walk back from the bow, the ring sparkling on my finger. We can't stop grinning at each other; I'm light and unsteady with giddiness. I feel as if a sword has been drawn out of my throat and the world has rushed back in.

Everything—everything—has been restored.

I bump Adrian with my hip. "So. We're getting hitched on the *Lair*, right?"

His face breaks into a series of irresistible dimples. "Naturally. And we'll have to come back here, so I can marry my Aurora under the aurora."

I glow, feeling ridiculously melty inside, and savor his nickname for me as if it has taken on a whole new, special meaning: "Your Northern Light." Then, switching to bantering humor again, "Naturally, Mrs. Colding will have to be the wedding planner."

"Naturally. How would we survive without her?"

We eye each other sidelong, bursting with happiness. I can't get over it. The thought keeps hitting me, over and over: *I'm his fiancée. I'm engaged to Adrian Voper. I am going to* marry *Adrian Voper.*

I have never felt prouder. To be with him. To be his. His woman.

Wait till I tell Mrs. Colding.

I don't have to wait long. There's a padding of soft-soled deck shoes, and down the starboard gangway hurries that distinctive silhouette: elegant, narrow-skirted, with that swan-like neck and severe upsweeping of hair. I'm lifting my hand with a smile—*Look, you did it, we did it, it's happened*—when I freeze. For Mrs. Colding's face, as it glides into the foredeck lights, is white with fear.

The feeling seeps into my gut like poison: *Something's wrong.*

She must have run here. She's out of breath, a fine sheen of sweat on her face. She presses a hand to her stomach as she speaks. "There was never a child." And she holds up a phone, Evangeline's phone, its display alight with a stream of texts.

Adrian stiffens beside me.

"She's been texting Volok," Mrs. Colding explains in a rush. "She lied to you. She was never pregnant."

Adrian takes a step back, his hand lifting to steady himself. He shakes his head once, futilely. "That can't—"

"Adrian." She fixes him with her eyes. "She was his pet all along. He sent her here to manipulate you into joining the coven again."

All the muscle tone goes out of Adrian's face.

But I don't hear this—because my eyes are trying to make sense of what's behind Mrs. Colding. Something is moving. Something is crawling down the side of the boat, a glowing white dress spread out behind it like the wings of angels. It clings to the polished fiberglass of the *Lair* like a lizard, nose scenting the air. It moves in sudden, jerky movements, as if time were stuttering.

The hairs on the back of my neck stand on end.

But I don't have time to move, to do anything more than make a funny wheeze, a kind of sad rattle. For the thing has flowed onto the deckhead running above Mrs. Colding's head, hanging upside down, and scuttles straight toward her.

I grip Adrian's arm, fingers digging through his sleeve into flesh.

"You have to hurry," Mrs. Colding says. "I think she saw me snooping—"

And Adrian sees now. His whole body tenses. The words come out of him in a ragged shout. "*Mrs. Colding!*"

She cocks her head; that's all she has time for. Because Evangeline Voper has stutter-flowed right above the chief stewardess, and letting her upper body fall away from the deckhead so that she's hanging straight down by the knees like some monstrous bat, she seizes hair and shoulder and nuzzles a mouthful of fangs into Mrs. Colding's neck.

All the oxygen leaves my lungs.

I feel it as a kind of physical jolt, an unthinking flinching away. My pulse hammers behind my eyeballs, making everything twitch. My insides knot into a sick, bunched feeling as blood gushes in a glistening fount down Mrs.

Colding's button-down, the white cotton blooming a lurid red. Her eyes widen as if she were in the grip of a miracle worker.

I hold a hand to my mouth, tasting a hot surge of vomit in the back of my throat.

Then Mrs. Colding is kneeling on the foredeck, blinking and brow drawn in confusion, one hand held to her neck with the blood pumping in lazy ebbs through the fingers. As if not yet understanding how her world has changed.

How my world has changed.

That glowing white shape drops down, and Evangeline rises to malevolent height behind Mrs. Colding, head thrown back and eyes rolled up as if in orgasmic relish of a prime rib steak. "*God*, I've been wanting to do that," she groans, chin bathed red and dripping, and smiles dreamily at the sky like a little girl whose birthday party has come early.

THIRTY-FIVE

I blink in place, and it's all still there before me. Mrs. Colding kneeling in her own blood. What has been done to her neck. And Evangeline standing over all like some dread conductor, smiling. Her virtuous choir girl's dress is freckled crimson. She looks like a bride from hell.

This isn't happening, I think. *This isn't real.*

Adrian seems to struggle with the same thought. He blinks as if he can't comprehend it, his eyes the widest I have ever seen them. He takes a staggering step forward, like a drunk in a hard crosswind. As if his heart, if it hadn't already, had stopped beating.

Somewhere far away there's a scream, a howl of such pure rage and grief it sends a chill down my spine. Then Captain Redfearn is charging past like a loosed bull, a vein pulsing on his brow like a fuse.

Adrian comes to life, dread like a live-wire in his voice. "Arnold, wait!"

Too late. Evangeline's arm blurs in a vicious, almost lazy backhand swipe, and all two hundred plus pounds of Captain Redfearn flies across the deck, crashing over a sunbed with a grunt.

The wrath finally grips Adrian. His whole body fills with it, a muscle twitching at his eye. He starts forward with hands clenched, but Evangeline grips Mrs. Colding's head by the hair and gives it a little shake. "Try it and I'll break her neck."

Adrian freezes, nostrils flaring. Evangeline sneers and looks up at the sky.

That's when we hear the faint *whup-whup-whup* of a helicopter.

Those sly eyes swing back to us, full of gloating spite. And Evangeline Voper begins to drag a half-conscious Mrs. Colding behind her, leaving a red smear on the teak deck, edging around us for the lit-up helipad.

Adrian's molars grind as he tracks her with his eyes. "Evangeline!" he snarls, then bites down on the fury in his voice, tries to smooth it out. "Evangeline. You don't have to do this."

I have, I find, sunk to my knees on the foredeck. When did that happen? My breath is short and labored. My hands tremble. As I watch Mrs. Colding's body slide past, I shake with fierce spasms of rage, with sounds too harsh to be grief. It comes to me, with foggy sluggishness, that I am out on the extreme edge of shock.

Then I remember: Captain Redfearn.

I crawl over to him on hands and knees, shivering as if I'd just dragged myself out of a lake. He's out cold, a nasty four-inch gouge carving across his brow in a faint gleam of bone. I feel his pulse. Still alive.

Then my eyes fall to the crew radio clipped to his belt.

The blood pounds in my ears.

But Evangeline knows exactly what I'm thinking. My hand hasn't strayed halfway to it before she lifts a finger. "Don't even fucking think about it."

I freeze, lips peeled back from my teeth, and share a look with Adrian. He has the exact same expression on his face.

He turns to her.

"So, it was all a lie," he grits out. His voice wavers, choked with the force of his disgust. "Even the baby." His clenched teeth shine white. His eyes are bright, as if he's close to crying. "Was any of it real?"

For the briefest of moments, regret flickers across Evangeline's face. Her response is so soft I can barely hear it. "My love was."

But Adrian only shakes his head at this, grasping at understanding. "Then *why?* Volok is your maker. If you help us end him, you'd be freed, too. You'd be free of all of this."

The whupping of the helicopter is swelling to a roar now. It's close, a gleaming black object gliding out of the sky, lights winking. But still, I can hear her cackle. It's the demented laugh of a madwoman.

"Oh Adrian," she croons. "You still don't know what you're up against, do you? You still don't know what he is capable of." She leans forward. "Even if we could pull it off, why would I? It would only take you from me." Her voice gets away from her on this last part, and she has to draw herself up again, undergo a reassertion of identity.

Her tone turns sly. "Besides, I never had any teeth in this world before." She shows a sharp and pink-stained smile. "Why would I give them up now?"

I watch Adrian take it in, the unavoidable truth: This is what she's become.

His face convulses, the corners of his mouth trembling; he can barely look at her. Then his gaze falls to Mrs. Colding slumped at Evangeline's feet. Her eyes wander, unfocused. She seems infinitely tired.

He swallows, jaw muscles flexing. At last, he lifts his hands, palms out in a calming gesture. "Just leave her out of it," he shouts over the noise, his tone careful. "Please."

Evangeline lifts her chin and looks down her nose at us, at the ring sparkling on my finger. Her lips peel back in a sneer. "Why throw eternity away for a child?" Her head juts forward, her shout over the chopper's blade slap almost a whisper, the breathy entreaty of a lover. "You could still come with me."

My stomach freefalls. I look to Adrian, my heart hammering against my breastbone. But the look he gives the woman he loved for over a century is both sorrowful and weary.

"Just leave her," he replies.

Evangeline blinks, eyes bright with held-back tears. Behind her the helicopter descends, a great black blur of shiny metal and whirling rotors. She glances back at it, her blood-soaked dress lofting in the wind like some gruesome banner, her hair a cloud of gold about her face. Then she looks back. I can hear it—the vital effort—in her voice. "I'll let the Commodore know your decision." And she hauls up a limp Mrs. Colding and tosses her toward Adrian.

My heart stops.

Adrian dives forward to catch her, and already Evangeline has flung the door to the helicopter wide. In the blink of an eye, a man in a pair of bulky headphones and a deckie's epauletted polo is hauled out of it, tumbling onto the helipad and skinning his hands, and the door shuts after her.

But I'm not concentrating on that. I've crouched down where Adrian has laid Mrs. Colding out on the helipad, and in a moment Captain Redfearn is beside me. He presses a washcloth over the ugly holes in her neck and brushes a stray lock of hair back from her face, his eyes swimming with tears. She looks a ghastly tint of gray.

When I look up at Adrian, I almost quail. The rage that has collected in his face—the pure, unadulterated vengeance—could destroy worlds.

"Arnold," he shouts in a bitten-off voice. "Radio the onboard nurse. And get a telemedical service on the satphone." Then he looks back to the helicopter that's starting to lift into the air, jaw clenching. "I'll be right back."

A tingling dizziness spreads through me. "Wait, Adrian—" But my hand closes on air.

I can't keep up with the pace of things now. Before I know what's happening, Captain Redfearn is shouting into the crew radio. The helicopter is lifting into the air, the revolutions of its blades as distinct as wingbeats. And Adrian is running flat-out to catch it. Cold dread shoots through me. I scream Adrian's name, bent over almost double from the force of it. But he doesn't hear me. The sound is lost in the hurricane of noise, and he keeps running. For a second, I think he'll miss it. The helicopter has begun to angle forward and is swooping past the bow when he leaps into the air—the breath catches in my throat—and manages to snag one of the helicopter's landing skids.

I watch on my feet, fingers in my teeth, as Adrian precariously swings from the skid. He hooks a shoe onto it and hauls himself up, crouches on it like a trapeze artist, his clothes rippling in the wind. He yanks at the passenger door with horrendous strength and rips it entirely away, unleashing a red blizzard into the air. Roses. The pilot must have been coming in with a delivery when he was told to pick up Evangeline.

Then Adrian has climbed inside, lost to view. And for a moment the old me thinks, *There they go. Leaving me at last.*

The helicopter veers wildly, as if drunk, and my heart pushes up into my throat.

No.

But it keeps veering, spinning into a death spiral, and my stomach drops as it plummets into the sea with a titanic splash, its rotor blades warping and chopping themselves up as they hit the water like a wilting black flower. Then silence.

A piercing pain stabs at my eyes. My knees threaten to give out. The world, for a moment, blurs and refocuses.

I whirl to Mrs. Colding.

Crew members have dashed out and lifted her onto a gurney. Her eyes are open and lucid. She looks up at me with a wan smile. "Go."

I open my mouth to argue, and she says it again. "*Go.* I'll be fine." And those cobweb lines draw up in a gentle smile. "Bloodsucking Barbie Bitch can't get rid of me that easy."

I bark out a harsh, helpless laugh and squeeze her hand. "Thank you," I whisper, and turn to Captain Redfearn. "You take care of her."

And turning to the pilot who's risen, agog, with headphones in hand, I snap him into action. "Get the tender! *Now!*"

THIRTY-SIX

They've barely got the limousine tender out of the garage before I've jumped in and revved it round the *Lair* and straight toward the wreckage, the freezing wind biting at my face. *Nothing's happened,* I tell myself, instinctively fingering the twinkling band on my hand. *I haven't lost him. I can't have.*

Unthinkable.

When I reach the crash site, I pull the kill switch and the tender coasts to a stop as I lurch to the gunwale, eyes sweeping the water. No helicopter; it's sunk out of sight. Only debris rides the waves. And petals, rose petals sprinkled everywhere, as if some fantastic world had been disgorged in the destruction of the chopper. The last performance of Evangeline Voper.

No sign of either of them.

"Adrian?" I screech. "*Adrian?*"

In the middle of all this, it's somehow not beyond me. The thought can occur: *This is what would happen. This is exactly what she'd want.*

How horrific. That even his vengeance would play into her hands.

Even in death, he still belongs to her.

But I push this away. I will not acknowledge what is waiting in my mind. I will still not allow myself to acknowledge it. The possibility. Adrian, gone. Her locking him in a final, cold embrace, sinking into gloomy fathoms. I have come too fucking far for that.

I'm starting to pull my parka off to dive in after him, hypothermia be damned, when a hand pushes up out of the water and slaps onto the gunwale.

I croak out a sob I'd not known was there and grab him, and with his sluggish help I haul him aboard and we collapse onto the floor of the tender. I can't help it—for a moment I have to crush him to me, as if to convince myself. *He's here. This is real.* Then he pulls back to give me a wild and anguished look, and I see there, naked and terrifying, the unutterable—what can never be said.

He's killed her. Killed his old love.

And more, the cost of it. What it cost him to do it. And I know: There are only a few moments like this in life, if they ever come, that there is this kind of helpless honesty.

"I," he croaks. "I—"

But I shake my head—*You don't have to say it*—and it's as if I've given him the permission he needs. The pain boils over. His chin quivers. Then he surrenders to it, in a harsh insucked breath of catastrophic grief, and I'm holding his wet body to me, pressing his face fiercely between my breasts. He clutches onto me, wracked with sobs, and I hush him. "It's okay," I croon. "It's okay."

You did what had to be done.

After a long while his shuddering subsides, and I stroke his hair. I can smell, very faintly, the scent of roses on him.

We did it. We're free of her. She's gone.

And I can feel it now. The relief. It's like the hissing cauterizing of a still-raw wound, banishing all infection. A shadow left behind.

We've moved—at long last—into a fresh, new space.

Adrian takes in a deep, calming breath, and I hold him to me. His spiked and brambly hair, the sweet shape of his skull. The boat rocking beneath me, lapped by the waves, has a strange and secretive motion. But if I close my eyes and concentrate, I can feel as if everything around me has gone perfectly still.

THIRTY-SEVEN

As the tender floats into the marina in the *Lair*'s beach club, I ask the waiting deckhands the question that's burning inside me. "Where's Mrs. Colding?"

In the medical room. *(Right,* of course *yachts have medical rooms.)* Adrian doesn't bother changing out of his dripping clothes. He leads me straight to a gleaming, futuristic space decked out with more toys than a land-based hospital: X-ray machines, defibrillators, oxygen tanks, even a decompression chamber that looks like some high-tech coffin.

At the far end of the room Mrs. Colding lies on a hospital bed with her eyes shut, blood seeping through a bandage on her neck. A red-eyed Captain Redfearn sits beside her, holding her hand.

Dread lodges in my gullet.

The nurse is writing up her chart notes on a computer nearby. She's an alarmingly young-looking brunette in a yachtie's skirt and polo; she must double as a stewardess. When she catches sight of us, she visibly swallows and smooths her skirt.

"How is she?" Adrian asks.

"Stable. She's sleeping now. She . . ." The nurse clears her throat. "She had to have a blood transfusion."

My pulse slows. I can see now the patch of gauze taped to the crook of the captain's arm, and the bag of blood hanging upside down from a stainless-steel rack standing by the bed. A plastic tube, bright with shunting red fluid, snakes down and into an intravenous cannula taped to Mrs. Colding's right arm.

"A blood transfusion," repeats Adrian.

"Yes. It was touch and go there for a minute. She lost a lot of blood." "Uh-huh," Adrian says, nodding rapidly. "Okay."

Tears push into my eyes. I have to remember to breathe.

Adrian slips his hands into his trouser pockets and squinches his eyes shut, the skin around them wrinkling. "So how is . . ."

"She should be fine." The nurse speaks in the clipped, professional tone that all medical workers seem to adopt after a while. "There were no acute reactions, but the doctor I spoke with recommended she be hospitalized for further observation. A medevac chopper is on its way. It should be here in a couple of hours."

Adrian nods through this, mashing a palm to one of his closed eyes. "A transfusion," he says again, and sucks in a wild, ragged sound.

A lump rises in my throat. I rub Adrian's back as the nurse averts her gaze. "Yes. But again, she's stable. Very rarely there are life-threatening complications, but so far so good. Hold on to that."

"Okay."

The nurse hesitates, as if considering saying more, and adds, "I'll be right over here if you need me."

"Thank you," Adrian hoarses.

When she returns to her clipboard Adrian shakes his head, his face screwing up as he almost whispers it. "If I'd just sent Evangeline away sooner—"

"No," I say, heart aching, wanting to wrap my arms around him. "No, don't think like that. Don't think like that."

He nods, standing there for a long, still moment, then slides his hands down his face and sighs.

"Okay." And taking my hand, he approaches the bed.

I'm not ready for this. Not ready to see Mrs. Colding lying under a white hospital sheet on the inclined bed, looking powerless and, for the first time, her age. For it's never been her bone structure that's given her face its forbidding and unforgettable character—it's all in those stony eyes and her remarkable ability to convey withering contempt, ironic patience, conspiratorial wryness with a mere twitch of her lips. All that is gone as she sleeps, relaxed into a state that is both aged and infantile, and startlingly vulnerable.

Adrian rests his hand on Captain Redfearn's shoulder, and the skipper looks up to reveal the harrowing glimpse of raw grief in his stitched-up face.

It's a long night. Mrs. Colding's heartbeat on the monitor blips slow and steady, but her complexion remains the same frightening shade of gray. The captain falls asleep with his head resting on his forearm on the bed, still holding her hand.

When I know for sure he's out, I confer with Adrian in a whisper.

"Is Mrs. Colding going to . . . I mean, will she turn into . . ."

The edges of his mouth tighten in a frown. "Maybe. If enough venom got inside her. There's no way to know for sure until . . ."

"She wakes up."

He nods, and we both turn to watch the arcing scroll of her heartbeat on the monitor.

The nurse comes over again to check Mrs. Colding's vital signs. Satisfied, she removes the IV drip and walks out with the blood bag in her hands. It looks like some kind of drained, membranous sac. Adrian fetches a chair and sits at a remove, keeping watch without getting up once over the next two hours. I give him space, knowing he needs time to think. About what, though, I'm not sure.

When the nurse lets me know the medevac is nearly here, I go up to Adrian and touch the back of his head, my fingers curling in his hair. "It's time."

Adrian nods and takes a shaky breath, rises. A little unsteadily. He reaches out, finds my hand and squeezes it, his thumb brushing my ring. His eyes are on the heart monitor.

It blips on, like a metronome slowed down to the gravest tempo.

When he stands over the bed, his pale face softens. He lays a hand, very gently, on Mrs. Colding's shoulder. "Hey there."

Her eyes move beneath their lids, crack open. It takes an effort for them to focus on us, and for one, vibrating moment I wonder who will greet us, which version of Mrs. Colding will peek out of herself at her friends before her.

Then a sleepy smile pulls at her mouth.

"The lovebirds," she murmurs, and helpless grins break across our faces. Her heart monitor continues, color pushes into her cheeks. She looks over at Captain Redfearn asleep beside her, and her lips purse tenderly. Even she is not impervious to cuteness, it seems.

Adrian, however, is solemn, burning to share something. "The medevac will be here in a few minutes. There's something I want to tell you."

She makes a small, impatient noise. "If this is about my medical care, you needn't worry. I'll be back before you know it. This place will fall apart if I'm gone long, anyway."

Adrian's eyes glisten, a gentle smile curving his lips. He forges on. "Arie and I will have to run. The Nosferyachtu Club will be after us now."

"Right," she says in a brisk and officious manner. Back to business. "So do I meet you in Colorado, or—"

"We won't be meeting you."

Mrs. Colding blinks, as if confronted with the inconceivable. "What?" "You're not going."

Color floods her cheeks. An indignant anger rises. "Even if you go inland, you'll still need—"

"No, we won't."

"But—"

"Mrs. Colding."

"I'll still be able to keep up—"

"You're fired, Mrs. Colding."

The order rings in the air with stunning clarity. Mrs. Colding blinks, eyes sheening over with tears, and something in her crumples, making her suddenly look old and hurt. "Why?" she breathes in a small voice.

Adrian shakes his head—*no, no*—and takes her hand in both of his. "You," he says, gripping tight, and his voice cracks. "*You* are the most loyal friend I could have ever asked for." His face twists, and for the first time I see tears fall from Adrian Voper's eyes. "And I will *not* allow anything to happen to you because of that." And before Mrs. Colding knows what's happening, he has dipped his head like some old-world prince to place a tender, lingering kiss on the fine bones of her knuckles.

Mrs. Colding's bottom lip trembles. She sucks in an astonished sob and presses a hand over her mouth—overcome with a gratitude unforeseen, unbelieved-in, eyes trickling at the corners.

When Adrian lifts his head, he wipes at his face with a palm. "Of course, you'll get the severance package you deserve," he says shakily, and clears his throat. "Suffice it to say you'll never have to work again. Knowing you, however, you won't have any patience for retirement. So you'll just have to find someone else's life to run." He grins and cuts his gaze sideways, and everyone turns to see that Captain Redfearn is awake, has been watching all this with red-rimmed eyes. "Like this guy's."

And we all look at each other, smiling—family—as the approaching roar of a helicopter fills the world.

We wheel her out on a gurney to the bulky medevac chopper waiting on the helipad. The cross emblazoned on its side gleams blood-red in the lights of the *Lair*, the force of its rotors flattening

our hair. As its heavy door slides back and the EMTs hop out, we all pause, recognizing the momentousness—the finality—of the moment. We don't know what to say.

Captain Redfearn doesn't say anything. He lunges forward, before he loses his nerve, and plants a rough kiss on Mrs. Colding's lips.

Adrian and I suppress grins.

When the captain pulls back, Mrs. Colding is blushing like a schoolgirl. "I'll see you soon," Captain Redfearn shouts over the roar of the chopper, and she nods, eyes shining.

Adrian steps forward, and she grips his hand till her knuckles show white.

Then she turns to me.

There's so much I want to tell her. So much I wish I'd said before. *Thank you for believing in me. Thank you for your friendship. Thank you for giving me the love of my life.* But there's no time for that. She beckons, and I lean close so she can rush a single, haunting sentence into my ear, my hair whipping in a tornado about us both.

"Remember: Never stop fighting."

I jerk back to look into her eyes, brow furrowed. Did I hear her right? But the EMTs have already lifted her up, and the door is sliding shut when she gives a last, enigmatic twitch of her lips and calls, "And I *will* be planning your wedding." Then the helicopter is rising into the air, whumping away in a cyclone of noise, and profound silence once again descends on that frozen dome at the top of the world.

It's a long time before Captain Redfearn sighs. "Well. I suppose I should chart a course for North America."

"Yes." Adrian tugs at my arm, but I don't move. He exchanges a look with the captain. "Come on. Volok will be sending his entire fleet after us now. We have to run."

Run. Yes. Isn't that what I've done all my life? Shouldn't that be easy by now? Why not live out the rest of my life in that mansion in Colorado, with its high rock and endless snows, cold as a vampire's heart? Do I *really*, in the end, need to free Adrian?

And yet.

I can hear it still, like an echo, breaking through this shiny, precious deception: what Mrs. Colding said. Reverberating in my mind like a past self, unwilling to be forgotten. Blowing cool puffs of confidence into me.

Never stop fighting.

Not just encouragement. A challenge. A riddle daring to be solved. Daring me to be what she always wanted me to be.

I walk to the bow, looking out at the formidable vastness of arctic sea and the huge shapes of icebergs, where far off the light of the helicopter hangs suspended like a guiding star. Maybe this is what she meant. This is the moment. This is the moment I'll know what has to be done.

Promise me.

I promise, Mrs. Colding.

And I lift my chin, breathing fog in the cold. "Yes," I say at last. "You'll have to run."

It takes a few moments for Adrian to register what I've said. The distinction. The bewilderment deepening, making itself known in his voice. "What do you mean?"

I haven't said it aloud yet. I can still turn back. It is still *before*. But I know I can't do that. The plan has taken root, sprung to magnificent, diabolical life in my mind, fed by a sweet trickle of vengeance. Adrian may have taken care of Evangeline, but I know who's truly responsible for the attack on Mrs. Colding. That shadowy figure would go on abusing and killing women, as was its nature, and there would be no escape until it was taken care of, too. No avoiding the night when cold shapes would drift out of the skirling snow to our door in the Rockies. No chance for Adrian and I to be together. No end to all of this.

So I take a deep breath in and say it.

"Volok will be after you. But even if Evangeline told her about me, he doesn't know what I look like, does he?"

Adrian cocks his head. "So?"

A shivery grin crooks my lips, and I feel a sudden urge to laugh. "So, remember what that stewardess from the *Neck Romancer* said? That the crews work both Volok and Radomir's boats?"

Adrian exchanges an uncertain look with Captain Redfearn, his voice slow with dawning realization. "Yeah?"

"Well," I say, lovely terror filling my chest, goading me on. "That means you'll have to hide, babe. But I'm going to end this." And I turn about to face him and the captain on the helipad of the *Lair* in that freezing waste, chin chucked up and riding a cool wave of clear-eyed fury. "I'm going to infiltrate Volok's boat as a stewardess and take him out myself."

READ ON
FOR A
SNEAK PEEK
OF
LAIR RECKONING

ONE

We see the polar bear an hour before dawn.

The other sights came thick and fast as we kayaked in the freezing sea off Svalbard. First were the seals and penguins hunting for fish, sleek shapes diving under the rippling blur of the water. Then walruses bathing on icebergs like tusked curmudgeons, their garrulous barks making us laugh. At one point the marbled vastness of a whale breached high in the air, so close its crashing splash rocked our sea kayaks and soaked us with its spray, making me gape with awe. But there's something different about the bear, something noble and rare. It stands on an ice shelf, watching us with its beady black eyes as we float past. It must weigh over a thousand pounds, its fur as white and fluffy as the snow around it, its forepaws as big as my head. It lifts its snout to scent the air (it's probably never smelled the undead before), then turns and shambles off into the freezing gloom.

I can't help but take its sighting as a sign. An omen.

Everything will turn out all right.

I rest my paddle across the kayak and look up at the Northern Lights.

It's impossible to get used to them. They hang in the gloaming sky in a shimmering, dancing aura of many colors, so close I feel I can reach out and touch them, pull their magic inside me. The north glows with it, reflecting it in the smooth glass of the sea, on the slopes of the snow-capped mountains—a mysterious half-light that makes it seem as if day never truly leaves this place. The land of the midnight sun.

This is what I'd needed. After everything that had happened in the past week, I'd needed a breather. A moment to decompress before plunging into the next terrifying step before me. And Adrian, of course, had known this. He'd arranged this date without fuss or letting me know what was up, and I'd only grasped it when he'd led me down to the stern of the *Lair* in the gloom of the predawn hours, and I'd seen the two kayaks waiting for us in the water.

I hear the almost noiseless stroke of a paddle, and another kayak noses up beside me. "It's hard to get used to them, isn't it?"

"Yes," I grin, my breath puffing fog in the cold.

There's no answering fog of breath beside me. "Now you know how I feel."

I roll my eyes. "Oh *God*."

He laughs, an achingly gorgeous sound in that untouched wilderness.

"Jesus, you've gotten *so* corny," I groan.

I don't mind, though. I don't mind at all.

I finally turn to look at Adrian Voper. In the enchanting half-light, I can make out the gleam of his creamy linen shirt (why bother dressing warmly when you're undead?), the sleeves of which are rolled to the elbows to expose forearms corded thick with muscle. The look in his vivid blue eyes makes my heart stumble, and his dark, brambly hair makes me want to run my hands through it. I settle for reaching out and taking his hand.

"My Northern Light," he whispers through crooked lips, his face glowing white as the polar bear, and now it's hard to breathe for the tightening in my throat.

His bare thumb brushes my engagement ring under my warm mitten. It was only days ago that he'd knelt under these same lights and revealed that ring to me. It still doesn't feel real. How is all this not a dream?

It takes me a moment to realize that the shivering of my body is not solely from my feelings for Adrian Voper. I'd bundled myself up like a cartoon character—thermal underwear under a wetsuit, fleece jacket, kayak vest and life jacket, neck warmer, thick wool socks and hat—and somehow I'm still freezing. I'd long ago accepted I was cursed with a poor circulatory system, but seriously? *Right now, Arie?*

Adrian has a solution for this too, though. "Hang on," he says and rummages through the cockpit of his kayak. In a flash, he's produced a silver thermos, and prying off its lid he holds it out to me with the shyness of a boy presenting a school paper. Steam coils out of it into the frigid air. "I thought you'd appreciate some hot chocolate."

My mouth does something between a pout and a sob. *How has he become so adorable?*

But there's more. "Wait!" he says, lifting a pale finger, and rummages into his cockpit again before he drops a few puffy white cubes into the thermos. "Can't have cocoa without marshmallows," he says simply.

I'm officially in a state of shock as I cradle the warm thermos in my mittens. It's hard to even recognize this Adrian beside me. How could this be the same Adrian who once fired staff for the slightest infraction, who couldn't see beyond himself other than to demand perfection from everyone around him?

I'd changed that. I'd done that.

He'd done it for me.

But it's more than that. No guy has ever treated me like this. No guy has ever made me feel this special and taken care of.

No guy has ever made me feel safe.

Adrian sees it coming. He tilts his head and purses his lips. "Oh baby," he soothes, checking the hot prickling behind my eyes. "Careful now, your tears will freeze."

I hiccup a laugh and shake my head, wipe clumsily under my eyes with a mitten. Then I take a sip of scalding sweetness from the thermos to distract myself, letting its warmth spread through me.

Adrian, mouth crooking gently, pulls my kayak close and rubs my back. "I can't wait to be human so I can warm you up."

"I'm looking forward to that, too," I quip, teeth chattering. "In more ways than one."

He shoots me a sidelong look, and we both burst into laughter. I laugh so hard, so freely, I have to gasp to get enough air into my lungs. By the time I'm done they feel rimed over with frost and I have to take another sugary mouthful of cocoa to thaw them out.

Then we're bobbing on the sea in silence, listening to the warbling of vast colonies of birds nesting on the cliffs.

I know without asking that we're both thinking the same thing. The next step. What I'd told him.

Me. Going after the Commodore. Alone.

It's been an unspoken tension between us ever since I first announced it, and I've been amazed he hasn't pursued it further. But I know it's coming now.

He doesn't try to talk me out of it, though. At least, not in the way I'd expected.

"You don't have to do this, you know." His voice is so low I can barely hear him. He's staring at his paddle athwart his kayak before him. "You could find someone human and not have to risk your life for me—"

"Don't say that," I blurt, voice edged with anger. "Don't ever say that."

He nods, takes a breath and looks up at the miles of white mountains ranged about us, the hyperborean spell above them. "I'm just worried. How could I not be? You going off, alone, to kill the head of our coven to free me—" He cuts himself short, checking a rising anger, the muscles in his jaws pulsing. "But I know it's your choice."

His knuckles show as he grips his paddle. "And I want you to have that."

I turn to look at him, that gratitude burning behind my eyes again. How hard it must be for him, going from controlling everything in his world to letting me go off on my own, beyond his reach, into the lair of his enemy.

"Thank you," I whisper.

He rolls his paddle slightly, watching the light catch on its carbon blades. "Just—promise me this won't change you, okay?"

"What?"

He still doesn't look up. "Please?"

Something about the stiffness in his voice, the vulnerability in his hunched shoulders, makes the hairs on the back of my neck prick. *What is going on here?*

"Hey," I say, tugging his kayak close. "Hey." I pull his face to mine, and our lips touch. He grips my jacket and breathes in, as if taking in as much of me as he can, leaving me dizzy. When I lean my forehead on his, he's shuddering as if—impossibly—he's been taken with a chill.

"You won't lose me, okay?" I whisper. "*Ever.*"

He nods, eyes shut. "Okay." And he smiles, that dazzling curve of teeth still able to make my heart soar.

We're still like that, kayaks bumping, holding each other brow to brow under the dancing lights of the aurora, when our crew radios crackle.

"You two aren't having sex on an iceberg or something, are you?" The unmistakable baritone of Captain Redfearn, resonant as aged oak.

I smirk and fetch the VHF marine walkie-talkie out of my cockpit. "You and your timing, Arnold." He's been grumpy as all hell since Mrs. Colding was medically evacuated a few days ago, and I've been doing my best to lift his spirits with the odd joke. But still. His reply is far more dour than I expect.

"Let's hope we have time for apologies later," it hisses over the radio.

The blood slows in my veins. Adrian and I share a look.

"Come again?" I tap the walkie-talkie.

"I'd get your asses back to the *Lair. Now,*" the captain urges. "I've picked up two incoming signals on sonar, only a few miles off. They're closing fast."

Adrian's eyes are wide. My breath coils in shivery veils of fog in the cold.

"I think it's them. The Nosferyachtu Club," Captain Redfearn continues, the dread thick in his voice. "They've found us."

**DON'T MISS ANY OF THIS EPIC SERIES
FROM D.V. SULLIVAN**

WWW.DVSULLIVAN.COM

ABOUT THE AUTHOR

D.V. Sullivan has been a deckhand in the Mediterranean, a bartender in New York and an English teacher in China. Now that he's no longer hosing salt off yachts during high-wind gales, he writes from his lair in the Pacific Northwest.

DVSullivan.com
Facebook.com/AuthorDVSullivan
TikTok @dvsullivanauthor
Instagram @dvsullivanauthor
X/Twitter @bydvsullivan

www.ingramcontent.com/pod-product-compliance
Lightning Source LLC
Chambersburg PA
CBHW061239310726

48971CB00007B/2139